JAKE MADDOX

HOCKEY RINK HEROES

STONE ARCH BOOKS
a capstone imprint

Jake Maddox is published by Stone Arch Books, an imprint of Capstone.
1710 Roe Crest Drive
North Mankato, Minnesota 56003
www.capstonepub.com

Library of Congress Cataloging-in-Publication Data is available
on the Library of Congress website.
ISBN 978-1-4965-9881-3 (paperback)
ISBN 978-1-4965-9882-0 (eBook PDF)

Summary:
Four action-packed hockey stories feature teens overcoming injuries,
rivalries, and other obstacles to achieve victory both on and off the ice.

Design Elements
Capstone; Shutterstock

Printed in the United States of America.
PA117

TABLE OF CONTENTS

HOCKEY MELTDOWN

HOCKEY MELTDOWN

CHAPTER 1
THERE GOES THE SEASON

Dylan Marshall stood on top of the skate ramp at Iron Valley Skate Park. He balanced on his skates and looked down at the pavement six feet below him.

His best friends, Nick Shaw and Tommy Reyes, stood on the sidelines, cheering.

"Come on, Dylan!" Nick yelled. "You can do it, man!"

Dylan wiped the sweat from his forehead.

Then, taking a deep breath, he used his back skate to push off. He shot down the ramp, picking up major speed. He reached the bottom of the ramp and flew across the pavement.

The wheels on his skates rotated rapidly as Dylan hit the next ramp. He kept his knees bent. As he reached the top of the ramp, he straightened his legs and jumped.

Dylan was flying. He kicked both feet to the right and reached down to grab his skates. His body whipped around in a complete circle. Then he released the grip on his skates and landed smoothly on the pavement. He skidded to a perfect stop.

"That was awesome!" Tommy yelled, skating over to Dylan.

"Thanks," said Dylan.

The boys skated over to a picnic table at the edge of the skate park and sat down.

"Can you believe school starts next week?" asked Dylan. He took a long sip from his water bottle.

"Ugh! Did you have to bring that up?" asked Tommy. He groaned.

"But if school starts soon, hockey season is just a few weeks away," Nick pointed out.

"I guess that makes me feel a little better," Tommy muttered.

"We're going to dominate this season," said Nick.

"Do you think we can win the Midwinter Meltdown Tournament?" asked Tommy.

"I know we can," Dylan said. "Nick can skate a lot faster than he could last year."

"And Tommy, you've been working on your backhand shot a lot, right?" asked Nick.

"It's golden," said Tommy. "And don't forget about Dylan's slap shot."

"His slap shot was already great," Nick said.

"Yeah, but it's even faster now," said Dylan. "I can't wait to get on the ice and knock a few shots into the back of the net."

"There's nothing better than firing a slap shot past the goalie," said Tommy.

"Nothing better," Dylan agreed. He jumped up from the table. "Except for maybe landing a 720. Watch this."

Dylan raced across the skate park. He skated back to the top of the tall ramp. Tommy and Nick both skated after him.

"Have you ever tried a 720 before?" asked Tommy. He sounded a little nervous.

"I don't know, man," Nick said. "Maybe this isn't such a good idea."

"I'll be fine," Dylan said. "Piece of cake."

With that, Dylan pushed himself down the ramp. He flew across the ground, up the smaller ramp, and into the air. He turned his body. He needed to do two full revolutions before landing on his skates.

The first spin was perfect, but the second one was sloppy. Dylan couldn't keep his body tucked in tight enough to complete the rotation. He was falling too quickly. The spin was going to be short.

At the last second, Dylan tried to rotate his upper body to finish the spin. Instead, the move threw him totally off-balance.

He crashed to the ground, landing hard on his right arm. Dylan hollered in pain. Tommy and Nick quickly skated over.

"Are you okay?" Nick asked. He crouched down beside Dylan.

"My arm hurts," Dylan said.

"Can you lift it?" asked Tommy.

Dylan tried to raise his right arm into the air. Pain immediately shot from his wrist to his elbow. "No, I can't," he said.

"I think it's broken," Nick said.

"It can't be broken," Dylan insisted. "What about hockey season?"

"Let's get you to a hospital," said Nick. "We can worry about hockey later."

"I can't believe it," said Dylan, flopping onto his back. "I just can't believe it."

CHAPTER 2

ON THE MEND

Ten weeks later, Dylan pushed through the large glass doors that led into the Iron Valley hockey arena. He looked down at his right arm. His cast had finally been removed. His arm looked pale and skinny compared to his left arm.

Dylan had missed the first few weeks of the hockey season. He was happy to be back.

It's been ten weeks, Dylan thought. *I just want to get back on the ice.*

As he walked toward the ice, Dylan straightened out his arm, twisting his wrist back and forth. He'd tried to practice using his hockey stick at home the day before. His arm still felt stiff.

"Dylan!" Nick shouted. Nick skated over as Dylan walked down the steps toward the ice. Their team, the Rangers, was in the middle of practice.

"The daredevil is back!" yelled Tommy. He skated toward the sidelines. A long plume of ice sprayed up as he stopped directly in front of Dylan.

"How are you feeling there, buddy?" asked Nick.

"Fine," said Dylan. "My arm is still a little weak, though. I'll definitely need to build up strength."

"When can you skate again?" asked Tommy.

"I can skate now," Dylan said. "But my doctor said I shouldn't practice with the team for another week. My arm needs to get used to being out of the cast."

"Bummer," Nick said. "But I guess a week isn't too bad."

"It means I can't practice until the Midwinter Meltdown," Dylan told his friends.

"That's okay," Tommy said. "We're awesome right now. We're undefeated."

"I know," said Dylan. "I've watched all the games from the bleachers, remember?"

"It's not like he's been living in a cave," Nick said with a laugh.

"Hey, guys! Bring it in!" Coach Erickson called from across the ice.

The entire team skated to the boards, where Coach Erickson was standing. Dylan walked over and let himself through the swinging half door to the bench.

"Let's welcome back our teammate," said Coach Erickson. The guys applauded. "I hear you still need to take it easy."

"Just another week," said Dylan.

"No problem," said Coach Erickson. "We can wait a week to have our slap-shot star back for the Meltdown Tournament."

"He'll be back, all right!" said Nick.

"And what about you, team?" Coach Erickson asked. "Are we going to beat the East Lake Scouts and bring home the trophy?"

"Yeah!" the team shouted.

"I can't hear you!" the coach yelled.

"YEAH!" the team shouted even louder.

"The trophy is ours!" Tommy yelled.
"We're going to win that thing and bring
it home to show our moms!"

Everyone looked at him. The team
was silent.

"Good one, Tommy," said Dylan.

The players broke out in laughter.

"Good to have you back, Dylan," said
Coach Erickson.

"Good to be back, Coach," Dylan replied.

CHAPTER 3

BACK ON THE ICE

A week later, Dylan, Nick, and Tommy walked into the arena where the Midwinter Meltdown was being held.

Thirty rows below them, a team was already out on the rink, practicing.

"That's East Lake," said Dylan.

The East Lake Scouts were skating in unison. When their coach blew his whistle, the players stopped, changed direction, and skated in the other direction.

"Their skating is perfect," said Nick.

"It's not that perfect," said Dylan. "We'll be able to handle them."

Privately, though, Dylan wasn't so sure. He still hadn't been able to practice with the Rangers. When he'd tried to practice at home, his arm had felt sore and stiff.

"Let's go, guys," said Coach Erickson, walking up behind them.

The Rangers headed to the locker room to suit up. When they got back to the rink, the Scouts were still there, finishing up the last of their drills.

"Is it my imagination or are they even bigger than last year?" Dylan muttered.

"What do they feed them in East Lake?" asked Tommy. "Steaks for breakfast, lunch, and dinner?"

"I just hope they don't eat us for dessert," Nick said.

The Scouts coach blew his whistle. The team skated toward the Rangers.

"Look at these runts," a Scouts forward said as he skated closer. "Are you guys sure you're in the right place? The preschool tournament is down the street."

"Is that Travis Caulfield?" Dylan whispered to Nick.

"That's him," said Nick. "He was the leading scorer in the state last season. And the big guy next to him is Peter Stevens. He's a defender. I heard he knocked three guys out of games so far this year."

"We're at the right tournament!" shouted Tommy. "And we're going to smoke you guys in the championship."

"The championship?" Travis repeated, laughing. "Did you hear that, Peter? They think they're going to the championship!"

"You guys don't stand a chance," said Peter. "Besides, even if you do make the championship, we'll skate circles around you. Just like we did last year."

"Not this time," said Dylan.

"It's a new year," said Nick.

"And a new tournament," said Dylan. "We're going to win it this year."

"Break it up, guys!" Coach Erickson interrupted. "Rangers, get on the ice!"

"See you at the championship," Travis said with a smirk.

"Oh, we'll be there," said Dylan. "And we'll beat you."

CHAPTER 4

BENCHED

Dylan skated backward across the ice. It felt smooth under the sharp blades of his skates. Nick and Tommy were beside him.

"Okay, guys," Coach Erickson shouted. "Let's do some warm-up drills."

"Feeling good, Dylan?" Nick asked.

"I feel great," said Dylan. "Like nothing ever happened."

"The three amigos are back!" said Nick.

"Enough talking, boys. Line up for the give-and-go drill!" shouted Coach Erickson.

The players took their places for the drill. Dylan and Nick lined up behind the goal, and Tommy skated out to the right circle. Another player lined up in the left circle, and two went out to the blue line. The Rangers goalie crouched in the net.

Coach Erickson blew his whistle. As Dylan watched, Nick passed the puck out to his teammate near the blue line. Nick skated hard toward the middle of the ice and received the pass back. Then he fired the puck quickly over to Tommy, in the circle, who immediately passed it back to Nick.

The puck hit the curve of Nick's stick as he skated toward the goal. He shot it hard past the goalie and into the net.

"Nice work, Nick!" Coach Erickson shouted. "Dylan, you're up."

Dylan's heart pumped. He couldn't wait to get the puck and blast it into the net. But he was nervous, too, and worried about his arm.

Coach Erickson blew the whistle.

Dylan quickly passed the puck to his teammate at the blue line. As he shot, a dull pain crept into his arm. He grimaced as he skated to the middle of the ice.

He passed the puck off to another teammate, and again, he felt an achy pain. "Ouch," he muttered.

Dylan pushed his skates hard off the ice and headed for the goal. He received the puck and flicked a hard wrist shot. Pain shot up his arm.

The goalie easily knocked Dylan's shot away from the net.

Shaking his head, Dylan took his spot back in the corner. *I have to get it together*, he thought. *We'll never beat the Scouts if I keep shooting like that.*

The team continued working on the give-and-go drill for several minutes. Each time Dylan tried the wrist shot, it was slow.

"Shoot it with power, Dylan!" shouted Coach Erickson from across the ice. "Let's see some speed!"

Dylan tried to shoot with the power he usually had. But his arm wouldn't cooperate.

Coach Erickson shook his head. Then he blew his whistle and called, "Slap shots! Line up for one-timers!"

Dylan skated across the blue line and over to the far boards. Coach Erickson stood on the blue line, near the center of the ice. He had a pile of pucks in front of him.

Coach Erickson flicked the puck across the ice. Dylan waited for it, raising his stick high into the air behind his body. As the puck cruised to him, Dylan pulled his stick down toward the ice.

Dylan's stick collided with the puck, sending it airborne toward the goal. It sailed smoothly into the back of the net. As his stick connected with the puck, Dylan felt the collision all the way up his arm. He closed his eyes briefly as pain shot from his wrist to his shoulder.

"Good one, Dylan," said Coach Erickson. He passed Dylan another puck.

Coach Erickson continued to pass him pucks, and Dylan fired shot after shot at the net. But each time he shot, the pain in his arm felt worse.

After several minutes of shooting, Coach Erickson held up his hand. "Nick!" he yelled. "Take over for me!"

Nick skated over and took Coach Erickson's spot in the center of the ice.

"Let's talk for a minute, Dylan," Coach Erickson said.

Dylan followed the coach over to the bench. Dylan took off his helmet and sat down next to his coach.

"I can tell your arm is still bothering you," Coach Erickson said.

"It's okay," said Dylan. "I'm fine."

"It's not okay if you can't play at full strength," said Coach Erickson. "Every player on the ice needs to give me a hundred percent."

"I can play," Dylan said. "I'll try harder. I'll keep practicing at home."

"I don't think so," Coach Erickson said, shaking his head. "I can't risk it. You could injure your arm more. And it wouldn't be fair to the team. I'm sorry. But I have to bench you for the tournament."

Coach Erickson stood and skated back to the center of the ice.

Dylan sighed in frustration and rubbed his arm. *Great*, he thought. *Now I won't help win the tournament.*

CHAPTER 5

WHAT'S THE POINT?

In the first game of the tournament, the Rangers took on the Apple Grove Muskies. Dylan didn't bother to suit up.

What's the point of wearing my uniform if I'm not going to be on the ice? he thought.

It killed him to be on the bench as his teammates spilled onto the ice.

"We're going to win this one for you, Dylan," Nick said.

"And the championship too," Tommy added.

"Whatever," Dylan muttered.

Tommy and Nick both skated out and took their spots as forwards. Dylan watched from the bench as the referee dropped the puck at center ice, and the game began.

The action was slow as the teams tried to get the feel of the ice under their skates.

No one scored in the first two periods. With only five minutes left in the third period, Nick and Tommy teamed up. They flew down the ice, skating hard, with only one Muskies defender to stop them.

Nick passed Tommy the puck, and Tommy passed it right back. It was just like the give-and-go drill they had worked on during practice.

Nick received the puck and charged hard toward the right side of the net. With just ten feet between him and the goalie, Nick faked a pass to Tommy on the left. The goalie fell for the fake. He lunged to the left, leaving the entire right side of the goal wide open. Then Nick flicked an easy wrist shot into the back of the net.

The final two minutes of the game ticked away on the clock. The Muskies tried desperately to even the score, but they couldn't get past the Rangers' defense. As the buzzer sounded, Dylan glanced up at the scoreboard: 1–0, Rangers.

The Rangers celebrated their victory on the ice. Dylan stayed on the bench.

A SECOND CHANCE

Game two was the next afternoon. Again, Dylan kept to himself on the bench.

The Rangers played even better than in the first game. They easily beat the Maple Park Orioles 3–1. The powerful scoring duo of Nick and Tommy was hard to beat. Nick scored two goals for the Rangers. Tommy scored the other.

After the game, everyone celebrated the victory in the locker room.

"We're going to the championship!" Nick cheered.

"Just like we said we would," said Tommy.

"I wish I could be out there tomorrow," Dylan mumbled.

"You should talk to the coach," said Nick. "Maybe he'll change his mind and let you play."

"Yeah, we could really use you, man," Tommy agreed. "Even if you're not at full strength."

Dylan rubbed his arm. "Maybe you're right," he said.

Dylan walked over to where Coach Erickson was standing.

"What's up, Dylan?" the coach asked.

"I want to play tomorrow," said Dylan. "My arm feels a lot better. I want to be out there on the ice with my teammates. I want to help them beat the Scouts."

"That's not a good idea," Coach Erickson said with a sigh. "I know you want to play. But you've only had one practice with the team since your injury. I can't just put you into the finals with no practice."

"But I've been practicing at home," Dylan said. "And I've been to every single Rangers practice and game. Even if I haven't been skating, I've been paying attention."

Coach Erickson thought for a minute. "Is your arm really feeling better?" he asked.

"Yes," said Dylan. "I wouldn't ask to play if it wasn't."

"I'll tell you what," said the coach. "Warm up with the team before the game tomorrow. If your arm is okay in warm-ups, we'll talk about you playing. But you have to tell me the truth. I don't want you to get hurt."

Dylan's smile covered his face. "You won't regret this!" he said. Then he raced over to his friends.

"What did he say?" asked Tommy.

"I'm in!" Dylan said.

"All right!" said Nick. "Now we'll beat those Scouts for sure!"

CHAPTER 7

TOO RISKY

The next afternoon, the Rangers warmed up on the ice. Dylan skated easily as he and his teammates glided in circles to warm up their legs.

Around the rink, other teams were warming up too. Dylan could see the Scouts skating nearby.

"Well, if it isn't the pipsqueaks from up north," said Travis Caulfield as he skated past.

Peter Stevens skated behind him. "Your opponents must have been a joke," he said. "I can't believe you guys made it to the championship game."

"Believe it!" Dylan said. "We made it here, and we earned it."

"Your team might have earned it," Travis said, "but you didn't. I heard you watched both games from the bench."

"That's enough, boys. Slap shots!" yelled Coach Erickson.

The Rangers quickly formed a line for the slap-shot drill. Dylan took a spot behind Nick. His arm didn't hurt, but he was still nervous. He didn't want to go first.

Nick took five passes from Coach Erickson and nailed five wicked slap shots into the net.

"Dylan, you're up!" the coach yelled.

Dylan skated into position. He looked at his arm. Then he closed his eyes for a second. "I can do this," he whispered.

The coach hit a slow wrist shot. Dylan raised his stick and swept it toward the puck. His stick and the puck met in a solid collision that he felt all the way up his arm. Dylan grimaced, but kept quiet.

Coach Erickson narrowed his eyes. "How's that arm?" he asked.

"It's okay, Coach," said Dylan. "Give me another one."

Coach Erickson frowned, but he fired another puck to Dylan.

Dylan wound up and shot the puck hard. This time, he couldn't help grabbing his arm in pain.

"That's enough," the coach said. "Your arm isn't better. Take a seat on the bench."

"No way," said Dylan. "I can do it."

"On the bench!" Coach Erickson yelled. "Not another word!"

Dylan threw his stick on the ice and skated toward the bench. He dropped down and put his head in his hands.

Nick skated to the bench with Dylan's stick in his hand. "Here you go," he said.

"I can't believe he benched me again," said Dylan, grabbing the stick.

"Your arm isn't ready," Nick said. "You know that."

"You're on Coach's side?" Dylan asked angrily. *I can't believe this*, he thought. *Even my best friend doesn't want me to play.*

"I'm not on anyone's side," Nick said. "I just think the coach has a good reason for keeping you out of the game."

"Oh, yeah?" muttered Dylan. "Why?"

"He doesn't want you to hurt your arm," said Nick. "And . . ." He looked away.

"And what?" asked Dylan.

Nick looked at Dylan. "The team might be stronger if you're on the bench," he said.

"Really?" asked Dylan. "So that's how it's going to be? You think the team will do better if I'm not playing?"

"I didn't mean it like that," said Nick. "But if you can't pass well and shoot hard, someone else can do a better job."

"Thanks a lot," said Dylan. "I thought we were friends."

"We are," Nick said. "And I thought you were a team player."

"Just leave me alone," Dylan snapped. "If you guys don't need me, maybe I should just go home."

"We need you, Dylan," said Nick. "We need your eyes from the bench. You can still help us win."

"Whatever," Dylan said. *Obviously Nick doesn't think I'm good enough,* he thought angrily.

Nick stared at him for a moment. Then he shook his head and skated back onto the ice.

Dylan slumped back on the bench. He watched as the teams prepared for the game. *I shouldn't have even put on my jersey,* he thought. *What a waste.*

CHAPTER 8

MIDWINTER MELTDOWN

In the first period, the Scouts were like a machine. They skated easily around the rink and scored an early goal. The Rangers tried to keep up, but the Scouts were bigger and faster.

Dylan didn't cheer for his teammates at all. He was too angry. He was angry with Coach Erickson for benching him. And he was angry at his friends for not supporting him.

Most of all, Dylan was angry with himself. He knew Nick was right. The team was better off with him on the bench. But he was upset to be missing the championship game.

After the first period, the Scouts led 1–0. Between periods, Coach Erickson talked to the team in the locker room.

"Guys, we're not skating as hard as we can," he said. "And our passing isn't as sharp as it should be. Lead your teammates down the ice. I want to see more shots. We can't score if we don't shoot. Am I right?"

"Right, Coach!" the team yelled together.

Coach Erickson looked at Dylan. "How about you, Dylan?" he asked. "Is there anything you've noticed that could help us win?"

"Nope," Dylan said. He shook his head. He knew he was being a bad sport. But he couldn't be enthusiastic when he was being forced to watch the game from the bench.

"Okay, guys," Coach Erickson said. "Let's tie this thing up!"

The players cheered. Then they started walking back to the rink.

Nick and Tommy cornered Dylan in the hallway. "We need to talk," Nick said.

"You're being a jerk," said Tommy.

"What are you talking about?" Dylan asked.

"I know you're upset you can't play," said Nick. "But you're part of this team."

"We need your help if we're going to win this game," said Tommy.

"You can see so much from the sidelines that we miss," Nick added.

Dylan was quiet for a minute. *Tommy and Nick are right,* he thought. *I'm being selfish. Just because I can't play doesn't mean I'm not a Ranger.*

"Well, there is one thing," Dylan said. "I noticed that Travis likes to skate to his right. If you cut him off and force him to his left, you'll throw him off balance."

"See! I told you you'd see stuff we didn't!" Tommy shouted.

"Thanks, Dylan," said Nick. "Keep the tips coming, okay?"

Dylan smiled. "Okay," he said.

Together, the three friends turned and marched back to the rink.

CHAPTER 9

A PART OF THE TEAM

As the second period started, Dylan was on his feet.

"Let's go, guys!" shouted Dylan. "Force the action! Crisp passes!"

The Rangers were much quicker on their skates in the second period. They were keeping up with the Scouts, and limiting their scoring chances. Nick was forcing Travis to his left every chance he got, just like Dylan had told him.

Five minutes into the period, one of the Scouts was called for tripping and sent to the penalty box for two minutes. That gave the Rangers a power play. They would have an extra player on the ice for two minutes. It was the perfect chance to tie the game.

Right away, the Rangers tried to score. Nick fired two different shots on goal. Tommy shot one at the net. But the goalie for the Scouts blocked all three shots.

"Keep shooting, guys!" Dylan called to his teammates. "One of them will go in!"

But after the two-minute power play, the Rangers were still scoreless.

The instant the penalty was over, the Scouts player flew out of the penalty box. Travis and Peter charged down the ice with him. Tommy and Nick were back to defend.

Travis had the puck on his stick. Peter danced around Tommy to the left, while Travis smoothly sailed past Nick to the right.

"Put a body on him!" shouted Dylan. "Don't go for the puck. Go for the body!"

Travis flicked an easy pass to Peter, who made the perfect shot past the Rangers goalie and into the net. The score was now 2–0.

"We need to put a body on them," Dylan repeated to himself.

With the Scouts ahead by two goals, they increased their intensity on defense. Peter lived up to his reputation as a hard hitter. He seemed to knock every Rangers player onto the ice. The Rangers had a hard time getting any shots on goal.

Near the end of the period, Nick made a rush toward the net. He looked back toward Tommy, who zinged the puck to him. Nick received the pass, then turned toward the goal. Instantly, he was met by a crushing blow from Peter. He hit the ice hard.

Dylan looked up at the scoreboard. The clock counted down. 3. . . 2 . . . 1. The horn sounded, signaling the end of the second period.

In the locker room, Coach Erickson tried to keep his team upbeat. "We still have one period to go, guys," he said. "We just need two goals to tie."

"Can I say something to the team, Coach?" Dylan asked.

"Um, sure, Dylan," said Coach Erickson. "Go ahead."

Dylan cleared his throat. "Here's how I see it, guys," he said. "The Scouts are skating around us because we aren't checking them at the blue line. We need to play the man, not the puck. We need to make some good, hard checks out there and knock them off their game. They like to skate. They don't like to hit."

"Peter likes to hit," said Tommy.

"Yeah, he does," said Dylan. "But so do you, right, Tommy?"

"Right," said Tommy.

"Then you handle Peter," said Dylan. "Stay on him this entire period."

"But the guy is built like a truck," Tommy said.

"You can do it, Tommy," Dylan said. "We all have faith in you. Right, team?"

"Right," the rest of the team echoed.

"And the rest of you," said Dylan. "Get physical and knock them off their game, okay?"

"Okay!" the team shouted.

The players stood and headed back toward the rink. Nick hurried to Dylan's side.

"Thanks, Dylan," Nick said.

"No . . . thank you," said Dylan. "Thanks for reminding me that I'm still part of the team. It doesn't matter if I'm on the ice or on the bench."

"Let's go win this thing," Nick said.

"Let's do it!" Dylan yelled.

CHAPTER 10

A TEAM VICTORY

At the start of the third period, Travis and Peter passed the puck back and forth across the blue line. Nick and Tommy were back playing defense for the Rangers.

Travis flicked the puck over to Peter. Tommy had a chance to knock the puck away, but instead, he drove his body into Peter's chest. He slammed into him and knocked him off the puck.

"That's the way to do it!" shouted Dylan.

Nick swiped the puck with his stick and quickly passed it forward. Tommy skated hard down the left side of the ice, and Nick skated down the middle.

The Rangers player passed the puck back to Nick, who sent it across the ice to Tommy. Nick darted around a defender and skated toward the goal. Tommy flicked the puck back to him.

Nick received the pass, faked the goalie to his right, and swept across the goal for a backhand. The puck hit the back of the net.

"Goal!" shouted Dylan. He shared a fist bump with Coach Erickson.

The Rangers continued to take Dylan's advice. They were putting their bodies on the Scouts, and Tommy was shadowing Peter nonstop.

The strategy was working. The Scouts didn't get a shot on goal for the first six minutes of the third period.

The Scouts were getting frustrated. As Tommy took the puck down the ice, Peter swung his stick hard at Tommy's knees. The referee blew his whistle. Peter was called for slashing and sent to the penalty box.

"Nice," Dylan whispered.

The Rangers took advantage of the second power play. Nick skated behind the net as Tommy positioned himself in front of the goal. Nick faked out a player rushing toward him and passed the puck to Tommy. Tommy did a one-timer, meeting Nick's pass with an immediate slap shot.

The goalie never had a chance. The puck sailed past him into the net.

"Goal!" shouted Dylan. "It's all tied up!"

There were only two minutes left in the game. "No overtime, guys!" Dylan shouted. "Let's win this thing right now!"

The clock continued to count down as Nick, Tommy, and the other Rangers tried to control the puck. But on a bad pass from Tommy, Travis intercepted the puck. Only Nick was nearby to stop him from scoring.

"Force him left!" Dylan yelled.

Nick skated backward, staying in front of Travis. But Travis tried to skate around Nick and go right.

"Play the body!" shouted Dylan.

Nick waited for the right opportunity, and then lunged forward. He put his shoulder and elbow into Travis's chest, forcing him to the left and off the puck.

Travis lost his balance and stumbled. The puck was left wide open.

"Go, Nick!" Dylan shouted.

Nick reached for the puck and pushed it forward. He crossed the blue line. Tommy skated toward the right side of the goal. Nick fired a pass in his direction.

Tommy took two hard strides around his defender and blasted a wrist shot high above the goalie's shoulder. The shot was perfect. It sailed into the net.

"Goal!" shouted Dylan. He turned to Coach Erickson for a high-five.

Ten seconds were left on the clock. The Rangers were ahead, 3–2.

Dylan counted down as seconds ticked away. The final horn sounded. Everyone, including Dylan, stormed the ice.

"That was a team victory all the way!" Coach Erickson shouted. "Here you go, guys!" He handed the Midwinter Meltdown trophy to Nick and Tommy.

Nick and Tommy lifted the trophy high above their heads. "Dylan, get in here!" shouted Nick.

"You guys won it," Dylan said, shaking his head. "You deserve to carry it."

"We all deserve to carry it," said Tommy. "This is a team win, and you're part of the team."

Dylan lifted the trophy high above his head, and the team cheered. "We're the champs!" Nick shouted.

"And next year I'll actually get to be on the ice," Dylan said. "The Scouts won't know what hit them!

BACK-UP GOALIE

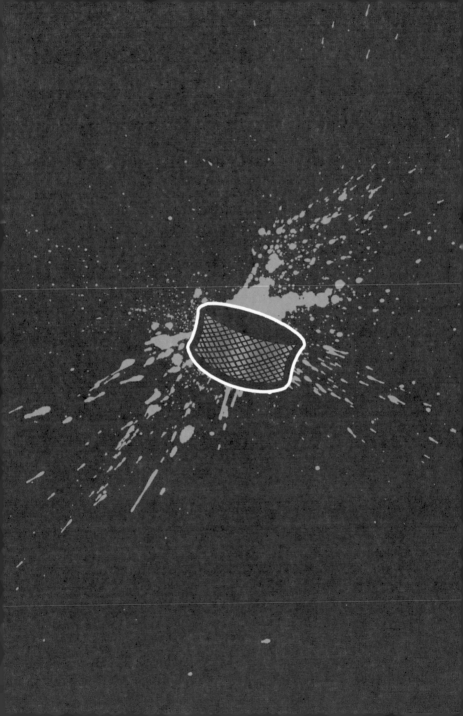

BACK-UP GOALIE

CHAPTER 1

READY TO GO

Jamie bent down and untied his skates. Then he carefully retied both of them, lace by lace. The hockey season was about to start, and Jamie wanted to make sure he was really ready to go.

The Comets' first opponents of the season were already out on the ice getting warmed up, but Jamie's coach kept his team in the locker room for a few extra moments.

"All right, boys," Coach Warren said.

Jamie's friend Jill cleared her throat. Immediately, Coach Warren got an embarrassed look on his face.

The coach quickly corrected himself. "I mean kids," he said. "Sorry, Jill. All right. It's time to hit the ice. The Spartans are going to be a big, physical team. Since this is the first year you are allowed to check in games, I know they will try to use their size to their advantage. But we have an advantage too, right?"

"Yeah, we've got the speed!" Jamie yelled out.

"That's right," Coach Warren agreed. "We'll use our quickness to avoid their checks and help us score. Now let's get out there and go!"

All the players got to their feet at once.

Most of them reached up and snapped their chin straps on their helmets. That made the locker room sound like popcorn popping in a microwave.

Jamie scanned the room.

Just about every player on the team was his size. That meant they weren't nearly big enough to be considered a physical threat on the ice.

The only exception was Brett, the goaltender. He was one of Jamie's best friends, along with Jill.

Brett was the biggest guy in their school. He was nearly a head taller than everyone else. He had a thick, big body too, so he really blocked the net.

It was tough for the Comets' opponents to get anything past him.

Brett was also one of the quietest kids in school. He was really shy, so he liked wearing the mask and all the padding in goal. It was sort of like wearing a costume.

The faster people fired pucks at Brett, the faster he blocked them and turned them away.

Brett had a great attitude about playing goal. It was a hard position to play, and there was a lot of pressure, but Brett was always calm. He never worried too much about goals he gave up, or anything that had happened in the past.

"I'll stop the next one," is the only thing he would say.

The Comets burst onto the ice and skated around their defensive zone, getting warmed up.

Coach Warren dropped a pile of pucks on the ice, and the players jumped into their pregame routine of drills.

As the Comets' forwards and defense players scooted around the ice, they fired pucks at Brett from all directions.

Brett would flip out a pad here, flash a glove there, or knock the puck to the corner with his stick.

Jamie kept an eye on their opponents, the Spartans, as he warmed up.

The Spartans were huge. Jamie felt like the other guys were twice his size. But as he had expected, they didn't seem as fast as the Comets.

Finally, the horn blared. It was time for the game to start. The Comets gathered around Brett at the goal.

As they always did, the entire Comets team stood together around the net. They crowded in around Brett.

Jamie was the team's captain, so it was his job to say something that would inspire the players.

"Okay, you guys," he said. "They might be bigger than we are, but they can't catch us. And we've got the ultimate big guy in goal. So let's go show them what the Comets are really made of!"

CHAPTER 2

STOP THE NEXT ONE

The Comets broke out of the huddle.
Then they skated off toward the bench area.

Most of the players gave Brett's huge leg
pads a swat with their sticks for luck before
they skated away.

Jamie was last. He and Brett had a
special routine they did before each game.

"Hey, big man," Jamie said, just like
always.

He skated around Brett as he talked.

"What are you gonna do?" Jamie yelled.

Jamie always hoped Brett would yell the next line. But he always just spoke it, calmly and quietly.

"Stop the next one," Brett said.

"And after that?" Jamie barked back.

"Stop the next one," Brett said.

As the referee's whistle blew, Jamie spun around in front of Brett and swung his stick at Brett's leg pads.

The pads thundered. *Thooomb!*

Brett didn't move an inch.

Jamie whizzed out to center ice. As the center on the first line, he would take the opening face-off.

Jill was the right wing on Jamie's line. A player named Marcus was the left wing.

Jill and Jamie had played on a line together since their second year in hockey.

The first year, Jamie played in goal. He struggled with the position, and he longed for a chance to use his speed.

Then Brett moved to town and wanted to play goalie. Jamie was more than willing to give it up.

Jamie had found his perfect position at center. Jamie led the team in assists almost every season. Either he or Jill always led the team in goals.

Jill had grown up playing with the boys, and she was one of the best players in the league. She kept playing with the boys even after a girls' program was started.

This year, since checking was allowed, Jill's parents had wanted to put her in the girls' league instead. They were worried that Jill would get hurt.

But Jill didn't want to switch to the girls' team. Plus, because of funding cuts, this year there were only two girls' teams. One team was for girls ages 12 and under, and the other was for girls ages 16 to 18. There wasn't anything for Jill, who was 14. So she ended up staying on the boys' team.

For five years, Jamie, Jill, and Brett had dominated the South Central League. The Comets had won the league championship every season. They had won the regional championship twice.

They had even gone to the state tournament and done well there too.

Their goal was to finally win the state championship. They felt that this could be the year.

Just as the referee got ready to drop the puck to start the season, there was a bunch of noise behind the Spartans' bench.

The Spartans' coach was yelling at the referee. The coach was waving some kind of booklet in his hand. He looked mad.

The referee skated over toward the Spartans' bench. As team captain, Jamie skated with him.

"I'm sorry, sir," the Spartans' coach said, "but is that a girl out there?"

He said "girl" like it was some kind of a bad word, Jamie thought.

Everyone looked out at Jill.

"Yeah, she's a girl," Jamie said.

"Well, I'm sorry, son, but she can't play in this game," the Spartans' coach said. He pointed at the booklet he held and added, "It says so right here."

CHAPTER 3

OFF THE ICE

The referee grabbed the booklet and opened it. Jamie read the cover: "The Official Rules of the City South Central Boys' Hockey League." The referee flipped through the pages.

"Here we go, Rule 7," the referee said. "Female players shall only be allowed to play if there is no girls' team available for them in the City South Central Girls' Hockey League."

By then, Coach Warren had gotten close enough to hear the conversation.

"That's right," he yelled. "That's the rule. And there's no Comets girls' team at her age level, so she's allowed to play with us."

The Spartans' coach was getting worked up. "But there are other girls' teams. And there are teams in the other leagues and in other cities that she could play on," he said. "It doesn't have to be a team here."

All the adults looked at each other. No one was sure what to do.

Jamie knew what he wanted to do, though. "Let's play hockey," he said. "You guys can figure this out later."

Seeing the adults arguing near the bench, the league's commissioner worked his way down to the ice.

The referee explained the problem and the commissioner looked a little confused.

"This is a new rule," he said slowly, "and I can see that it can be interpreted a couple of different ways. It's not very clear. I think for the time being, she should be held out of games. We need to sort this out." The commissioner crossed his arms.

Jamie groaned. He turned and skated out to Jill. He told her what was happening. Jill's head drooped.

As tough as she looked wearing full hockey gear, she looked like she might start to cry.

Jamie put his arm around her as they skated off the ice. "Don't worry, you'll be back before you know it," Jamie said. "They can't keep you away from the Comets!"

He wasn't so sure, but he wanted Jill to feel better. "And in the meantime," he added, "we'll win this game for you."

Coach Warren put Danny out to take Jill's place at right wing. Finally, they were ready for the game to start.

The referee dropped the puck.

Jamie and the Spartans' center jostled for it. Jamie pulled it free and dropped it back to a defenseman. The Spartans' center knocked Jamie to the ice with a bump.

Jamie scrambled back to his feet, wheeled around, and headed to the offensive zone.

The defenseman tried to feed the puck to Danny, but a Spartans forward intercepted it. They raced in on Brett and got off a quick shot. Brett turned it away with a pad.

The puck bounced to the corner. A Comets defenseman tried to get it, but a Spartans winger pulled it away. He centered it out front.

Jamie blocked the pass, but it deflected to a Spartan at the point.

For the next minute, the Spartans dominated the ice.

Brett made save after save, but the big Spartans team just kept coming.

Finally, the puck rolled to the corner. Jamie and the rest of the Comets were tired. They needed a line change. But with the puck in their end, they couldn't switch. They needed to force a face-off.

A Comets defenseman was battling for the puck in the corner. "Tie it up!" Jamie yelled. But the puck came free.

Again, it was fed out into the slot. Jamie tried to check the Spartans' center coming down the slot, but he was too big for Jamie to handle.

As they battled for position, they both lost their balance. They slid hard into Brett, and the puck sailed harmlessly away.

That's when Brett made a noise Jamie had never heard before.

Brett crumpled to the ground. His knee was bent to one side.

Jamie looked down. He saw that his friend was lying on the ice. Brett was screaming in pain.

CHAPTER 4

GO IN GOAL

Jamie and a couple other players helped Brett off the ice. Brett couldn't put any weight on his left leg.

Jamie couldn't believe what had happened to his day.

When he woke up that morning, he had been full of excitement. The Comets had another chance to win the Central League. They could make a run for the state championship.

Now, in less than five minutes, he had lost two of the team's best players and his two best friends on the team. Maybe even for the whole season. Everything had come crashing down around him.

When he got back to the bench after helping Brett to the locker room, Jamie's day got even worse.

"Jamie," Coach Warren said, "I need you to go in goal."

"Me?" Jamie exclaimed. "Are you kidding? What about Carlos?" Jamie knew they had another goalie. But then he realized he hadn't seen Carlos that day.

"Carlos is having trouble with his grades," the coach replied. "He's out for the semester. And you're the only one on the team who has played goalie before."

"But Coach, that was years ago!" Jamie said.

"Jamie, I need you in goal," the coach said again. His voice was firmer this time. "Go put on the equipment."

Jamie turned and marched back to the locker room.

The game was held up while he worked his way into the 30 pounds of equipment that Brett wore in goal.

The hardest part wasn't the weight of the gear. It was the size.

Brett's leg pads were huge on Jamie. The chest protector hung off Jamie's sides. He could barely move.

"This is ridiculous," Jamie muttered as he stood up to head back to the rink.

Brett already had a big bag of ice on his left knee. His father was there, getting ready to take him to the hospital for X-rays.

Jamie headed back to the ice. "Hey, Jamie," Brett called. "Stop the next one."

Jamie smiled. "Got it," he said. "Stop the next one."

But Jamie didn't feel like he could stop anything wearing all that equipment. He stumbled out to the ice and made his way to the goal crease.

That's when one of the Comets' defensemen came up. He whacked Jamie's leg pads, yelling, "Stop the next one!"

Unlike Brett, who always stood firm, Jamie crumpled to the ground. As he fought his way back to his feet, he heard some people in the crowd laughing.

Finally, the referee dropped the puck to start the game.

To Jamie, the game seemed to last forever.

He did his best to get in front of the pucks the Spartans shot. But in that huge equipment, it was really hard to move.

So, if the puck was shot right at him, he stopped it. If it was off to one side or another, he had no chance.

By the end of the game, the Spartans had put six goals behind Jamie.

Without Jamie and Jill on offense, the Comets managed only one goal. The season began with a 6–1 loss.

Jamie stormed off the ice. He yanked off the goalie equipment in the locker room. He was mad.

After each game, Coach Warren gave the team some pointers.

Today, he wrapped up his talk by saying a nice thing about Jamie. "That wasn't easy, going in goal like that," the coach said. "We should all thank Jamie for trying so hard."

Whew, Jamie thought. *At least I don't have to do that again.*

But Coach Warren had different ideas. "Jamie, come talk to me before you leave," he said.

CHAPTER 5

STEP UP

Jamie knew what the coach wanted to talk about. He just knew Coach Warren wanted him to go in goal again during the next game.

"Jamie, we're going to need you to play in goal until Brett gets back," Coach Warren said. "I hope that won't be long, but we need a good player in there."

Jamie sighed. Great. Now his day couldn't get any worse.

"But Coach, how are we going to score any goals without me and Jill at forward?" Jamie asked. "Wouldn't it be better to put someone else in goal, and keep me up on offense?"

Coach Warren wasn't about to budge. "Jamie, you're our captain," the coach said. "Without Brett and Jill, we're going to struggle. You and I both know that. But the rest of the team needs to believe that we can win. I need you to step up and be the leader of this team."

Jamie didn't know what to say.

He wanted to say the right thing, which was that he would do his best in goal and try to help his teammates.

But scoring goals was his favorite part of the game.

And if he was playing goalie, he wasn't going to do any scoring at all.

But he had to do what his coach said. So Jamie nodded at Coach Warren and turned to leave. "See you at practice," Jamie said.

CHAPTER 6

MORE BAD NEWS

When Jamie showed up at practice the next night, Coach Warren had a surprise for him.

"I borrowed a set of goalie equipment from a different team. I think it will fit you a little bit better," the coach said. "That should make your job as goalie easier."

Jamie found that the coach was right. The equipment did fit better. It was much lighter too.

That allowed Jamie to move better and more quickly, so he could get to more shots. And getting to more shots meant he was able to stop more shots.

Still, Jamie had a hard time during practice. The main reason he didn't let in many goals was that the shooters weren't doing a very good job.

Two nights later, the Comets were scheduled to play their second game of the season. This time, they would face the Badgers.

The Badgers were an average team in the league. The Comets usually beat them easily. The year before, they'd won by six points. But because of the Comets' new lineup and missing players, Jamie knew this year's game would be tough.

He wasn't looking forward to the game at all.

* * *

The day of the game, Jamie got some more bad news.

Jill stopped at his house after school to tell him what was going on. They didn't have any classes together, so she hadn't had a chance to talk to him during the day.

They sat in Jamie's room with sodas. "So, what's the scoop?" Jamie asked.

Jill sighed. "They aren't going to talk about it until the next board meeting, and that's two weeks from now," she said. "So until then, they put me on the Spartans' girls team. Can you believe that? Me, a Spartan?"

Jamie shook his head in disbelief.

"We don't have practice tonight, so I can come to your game," Jill said. "Brett's going to come too. Did you hear what the doctor said about his knee?"

"Oh, no," Jamie said, fearing the worst. "Not more bad news."

CHAPTER 7

NO CHANCE

Jamie braced himself for what he was about to hear.

"Brett's knee is sprained really bad," Jill said. "He can use crutches to walk, but I guess he's not going to be able to play for two or three months."

"Two or three months?" Jamie exclaimed. "That's more than half the season! I can't stay in goal that long!" He couldn't believe it.

"Come on, Jamie," Jill said, trying to sound encouraging. "It won't be so bad. All you have to do is win enough games to keep us in the running for the playoffs. Even if you only win half the games, we'll be okay by the time Brett and I get back."

Jamie didn't care. "Are you kidding me?" he yelled. "In two or three months, we'll be something like 0–20. Even if Wayne Gretzky came to play for us, we wouldn't have a chance!"

Jill laughed. She knew Jamie was being his usual nervous self. He was just imagining the worst that could happen.

"Just stop the next one," she said, laughing. "And then the one after that, too!"

BAD ATTITUDE

That night, when Jamie showed up for the game, he was in a terrible mood.

Usually, before a game, he was excited. He would laugh a lot, tell jokes, and get everyone else on the team excited too.

That night was different. Jamie wasn't excited. He got dressed quickly, slamming his locker door and stomping around.

He was a real grump.

He grumbled as he put on his gear. He whined as he did his stretching exercises. He growled as the team warmed up for the game.

Finally, the puck dropped to start the action. Jamie tried his best to focus.

But then the Badgers' first shot of the game snuck past him. It sailed between him and the left post for the game's first goal. The Badgers were already in the lead.

Jamie's attitude took an even deeper dive after that happened.

"This stinks!" he yelled out loud.

He slammed his stick against one of the goal posts. Then he yelled, "We don't have a chance!"

The rest of the game wasn't much better.

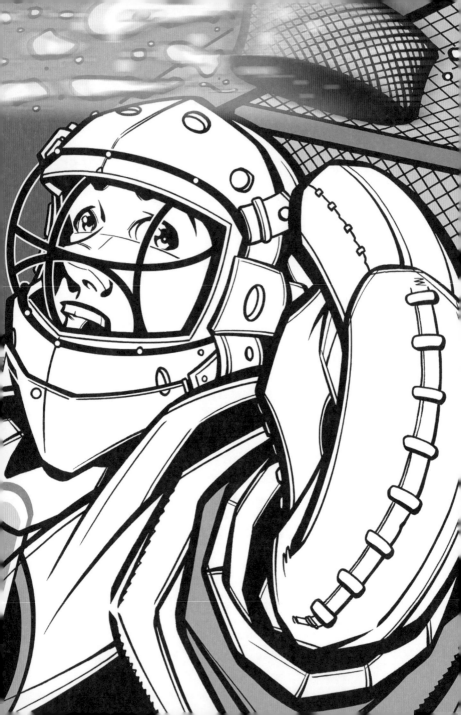

Jamie played better than he had in the game against the Spartans, but he still let four goals get past him.

Worse, the Comets offense couldn't put any pressure on the Badgers' net.

It was a total loss, 4–0.

Jamie couldn't remember the last time the Comets had gone an entire game without scoring a goal.

He wasn't sure it had ever happened.

After the game, Jamie didn't say a word to Jill and Brett, who had come to watch. He bolted straight from the arena and headed home.

At home, Jamie showered quickly and got into his pajamas.

All he wanted to do was close his eyes.

Jamie just wanted to forget about hockey for a while.

But before he got into bed, he heard the chime of his doorbell. A moment later, he heard his mother call, "Jamie, your friends are here."

Jamie's bedroom door swung open. Brett hobbled in on crutches. Jill was right behind him.

"Can you believe that game?" Jamie blurted out. He was feeling very sorry for himself. "Wasn't that awful?"

"Yeah, it stunk," Brett said.

Jill agreed. "Yep, terrible," she said. "And we think the worst part of the whole game was you."

CHAPTER 9

A NEW JAMIE?

Jamie wasn't sure what his friends meant.

Were they saying he was a terrible goalie? No matter what they meant, he was sure it wasn't good.

"Yeah, I didn't play very well," Jamie mumbled.

"Oh, it wasn't that," Jill said. "We actually think you played fine."

Jamie looked up. Brett nodded at him.

"It's your attitude that stinks," Jill said.

Jamie really wasn't sure what to do or say. He could feel himself getting very mad.

"What am I supposed to do?" he yelled angrily. "I'm playing a position I hate, and our team stinks. Before, we were a team that could have won the state tournament. Now we're a team that can't even score a single goal."

"I thought you were the captain of the team," Jill said.

"I am the captain," Jamie said.

"You're not acting like it," Jill said. "You're supposed to be helping everyone get better, not yelling and whining just because things got a little hard."

Jamie felt like his friends were attacking him. "What about you, Jill?" he said, crossing his arms and looking at Jill. "You came over and whined about playing for the Spartans girls' team."

"That's when I'm with you guys, in private," Jill said, shaking her head. "It's one thing to talk that way to your friends. It's another thing to take that to the game. That hurts your own team. When I'm with the Spartans girls, I try my best and don't complain. You're making us all look bad out there."

The room was quiet for a long time.

Finally, Brett spoke up. "We're still a team," he said to Jamie. "Jill and I aren't playing now, but that doesn't mean we're not Comets. When we get back, we want the team to still be together!"

Jamie looked at his friends. He suddenly felt very bad about the way he had acted.

But at the same time, Jamie felt a sense of pride. They were all still Comets. And it was up to Jamie to keep the team moving forward.

"Okay, I get it," Jamie finally said. "From now on, you'll see a new Jamie."

Jill and Brett laughed. "I can't wait to meet him," Jill said.

CHAPTER 10

CAPTAIN

The next night at practice, Jamie showed up with a smile on his face.

He walked right over to Coach Warren and asked if he could talk to him.

"Hey, Coach," Jamie said. "I brought my regular skates. I was thinking I could skate out tonight."

"No, Jamie," Coach Warren began. "You know we need you in goal until Brett gets back."

Jamie smiled. "I know, Coach," he said. "I've got an idea. For the first half of practice, let me skate out with the forwards. I can help them with handling the puck, and passing and shooting drills. Plus, that will give me a chance to keep my forward skills sharp for when Brett gets back."

Coach Warren's eyes lit up. It looked like he was beginning to like this idea.

"Then, for the second half of practice, I'll put the goalie gear on and work on my goaltending, and the forwards can shoot at a real goalie," Jamie said.

Coach Warren beamed. "That's the kind of thinking I like in a captain," he said. "Go ahead and get ready."

Score one for the new Jamie, Jamie thought as he put on his equipment.

Once the ice was ready for play, Jamie was the first player on it. When the rest of the team joined him, he led stretching exercises. He also filled the other players in on his plan for that night's practice.

When drills began, it seemed like Jamie was everywhere.

One minute he was skating to the net and making a great play of his own. The next minute he was explaining positions to a teammate or helping another with his passing.

Halfway through practice, Jamie skated off to change into his goalie gear. When he came back on, the smile was still on his face.

Even in goal, he was encouraging his teammates and calling out instructions.

Coach Warren barely had to say a word the whole practice.

The Comets' fortunes began to change almost right away. In the first game back, they scored three goals against the Muskies.

They lost the game 4–3, but the whole team left the ice feeling better.

The game after that, Jill and Brett came to watch. Jill carried a sign that read, "Go Comets! Go Jamie!"

Jamie smiled when he saw it.

That night, he had his best game yet in goal. He made 26 saves. The Comets tied the Bruins, ending up 2–2.

CHAPTER 11

LIKE OLD TIMES

Over the course of the next few weeks, the Comets kept getting better.

They won two games, tied two, and only lost one.

That left them with a record of two wins, four losses, and three ties heading into a rematch with the Spartans.

The night before the Spartans game, Jamie's phone rang.

"May I speak to the Comets' star goalie?" Jill said, laughing into the phone.

"Knock it off, Jill," Jamie said. But he smiled.

"Hey, guess what?" Jill said. She sounded happy. "I've got some good news for you. As of today, I'm a Comet again!"

Jill explained that after lots of arguing, the league's board voted to let her play for the Comets boys' team.

They finally agreed because she had been registered to play with the Comets, and there was no Comets girls' team at her age level.

When Jill returned to the Comets, she helped the team turn the corner. The rest of the forwards had already started to play a lot better.

Jill stepped right into the first line with Marcus and Danny. The three teammates clicked right away.

By the end of January, Brett's knee was healthy enough for him to return.

The Comets were right where they hoped they would be. They had ten wins, nine losses, and five ties.

Jamie was ready to jump right back in at forward, since he had been practicing all along.

Jamie showed up early for his first game back at forward. Then he looked at the lines Coach Warren had posted on the locker room wall.

He saw that his name was listed at center on the first line. Jill would be on his right, just like old times.

But Jamie had one more surprise for Coach Warren and the team.

"Hey Coach," Jamie said. "Why don't you put me on the second or third line? Jill's line has been doing great. I don't want to screw it up. Plus, then we'll have two good scoring lines."

"Still thinking like a captain, I see," said Coach Warren, smiling.

The coach made the switch. During the game that night, each line scored two goals.

A few months later, it was time for the Comets to accept their state championship trophy. And it was their captain, Jamie, who got his hands on it first.

FACE-OFF

FACE-OFF

CHAPTER 1

EAGLES VS.
ICE CATS

Kyle Parker sat on the bench as the hockey game was about to start. Eric, the Eagles' first-string center, was in the face-off circle. Connor was his left wing, and Dave was his right wing.

The ref dropped the puck, and Eric slammed his stick down. The puck flew to Connor. The game had begun!

"I can't wait to get out there," said Kyle, watching the action on the rink.

"You and me both," said Sean, his best friend.

"Yeah," said Kyle. "I'd be out there scoring as left wing."

"It's not that easy," said Sean.

"It is for Parker boys," said Kyle. "Look at my brother, Caleb. He's the top scorer in the league."

"Kyle, Sean, Chris," said Coach Williams. "Out on the ice."

"About time," said Chris, the second line center.

"Here we go," said Kyle.

The Ice Cats had scored.

Eric, Connor, and Dave came off the ice. Kyle, Sean, and Chris went in for their turn.

The three new Eagles players all skated toward the face-off circle in the neutral zone.

Chris skated into the circle to wait for the face-off. He knew he had to get the puck to Sean, his right wing, before the other team got it.

The ref dropped the puck.

Chris hit the puck out of the circle. Sean skated over and caught it right on the tape. The Ice Cats' wings skated over to Sean, so he passed the puck to Kyle. Kyle moved the puck into the offensive zone.

The Ice Cats' left defenseman glided toward Kyle. He tried to knock the puck away. Kyle did a deke. He pretended to move right, but then he passed left to Sean.

Sean caught the puck on his stick and moved toward the goal. The goalie moved back and forth in front of the net.

Kyle moved around the Ice Cats' left defenseman toward Sean. Sean passed the puck to Chris. Chris spun around and passed the puck to Kyle.

I got this! Kyle thought. He aimed at the goal. The Ice Cats' defenseman swept the puck away from Kyle.

"Hey!" yelled Kyle. He spun around and chased the player, but it was too late. The Ice Cat player passed the puck to his center who was gliding quickly toward the Eagles' goal.

Kyle skated after the Ice Cats' center. So did Sean and Chris.

"Check, double check," said Sean.

"Let's do it," said Kyle.

Kyle skated up behind the Ice Cats' center. Kyle reached his stick out and lifted the Ice Cats' center's stick. Sean came in from the other side and stole the puck.

Sean passed the puck to Chris. Chris skated across the blue line into the offensive zone. Kyle followed Chris on the left. Chris passed the puck to Kyle.

Kyle got the puck. Then he snapped his wrist, and the puck flew through the air toward the net.

The goalie leaped.

Just when Kyle thought the puck was going in, the Ice Cats' goalie knocked the puck away with his glove.

SECOND SHIFT GOAL

Kyle sat on the bench as the second period got underway. The Eagles' players were skating around the Ice Cats' net.

"Look at that!" said Kyle. "Connor missed! How could he miss a shot like that?"

"Everyone misses sometimes," said Sean.

"Not my brother, Caleb," said Kyle.

"I've seen him miss lots of times," said Sean.

"Yeah, but he scores a ton," said Kyle.

"Because he shoots a lot," said Sean.

"Kyle, Sean, Chris," said Coach Williams. "Out on the ice."

"Yes!" said Kyle. "Hey, Chris, hit it to me after the face-off."

"You got it, man," said Chris. He skated into the face-off circle in the neutral zone.

The ref dropped the puck and Chris slapped it out of the circle.

Here it comes, thought Kyle. He stopped the puck with his stick. Then he turned around and skated toward the offensive zone.

Kyle looked at the net. He saw an opening! He pulled his stick back and— *wham!* Slap shot!

The Ice Cats' goalie lifted his glove and caught the puck.

Man! Good save, thought Kyle.

"You should have waited until you were closer," said Chris as he skated past.

"Next time," said Kyle. "Hit it to me again."

"I'll try," said Chris.

On their next shift, Kyle's line won another face off. Kyle watched the puck fly toward him. *I've got to score!* he thought.

He glided closer to the net. The two Ice Cats' defensemen moved over to block the shot.

I can't shoot, Kyle thought.

He glanced at Sean. Sean looked open. Kyle figured that an assist was better than nothing!

Kyle moved his stick to sweep the puck over to Sean. Suddenly, an Ice Cat lifted Kyle's stick and stole the puck!

Kyle skated after the other player. He came from behind and lifted the Ice Cat's stick, stealing the puck back. *Two can play this game!* he said to himself.

Kyle spun around and skated back toward the net.

The defenseman was behind him, moving fast.

No time to waste, thought Kyle. *There are only two players defending the goal.*

Kyle swung his stick back.

Wham! Slap shot!

The puck sailed into the net.

The goalie missed!

I scored! thought Kyle. *Oh yeah!*

CHAPTER 3

BIG BROTHER

Kyle sat on the bench and looked out at the players on the ice. The Ice Cats had just scored on a power play. Their players outnumbered the Eagles on the ice five to four. They were now ahead of the Eagles for the second time that night.

"I'll never catch up with my brother's total by just sitting here," said Kyle.

"Look at that!" said Sean.

"Connor missed again. And Dave was a lot closer to the net."

"Connor doesn't like to share the puck," said Kyle.

"They're getting tired," said Sean.

"Yeah."

"Hey," said Sean. "Is that your brother over there?"

Caleb? Kyle looked up at the stands. "Where is he?" Caleb had never been to one of Kyle's games before. He was too busy playing center for the varsity team.

"That looks like him over there." Sean pointed.

Kyle tried to find his brother's face in the crowd. Then a whistle blew!

Coach Williams turned to the bench.

"Second line, get out there!" he said.

Kyle stood up and skated out onto the ice. There was no time to search for Caleb now. *At least he'll get a chance to see me play*, thought Kyle.

Chris and Sean skated out after him.

"Hit it my way, Chris," said Kyle.

"Go Eagles," said Chris, and he skated toward the face-off circle.

An Ice Cat hit the puck after the drop.

"Oh, no you don't," said Kyle, and he skated after the puck. The Ice Cats' left wing had it, so Kyle lifted the wing's stick and swept it away.

Watch this, big brother, thought Kyle excitedly. *I have the puck, and everyone else is behind me. Now I can score!*

Suddenly, Kyle saw a flash of white. He was face down on the ice.

The ref grabbed the puck and skated to the scorer's area.

"Tripping!" called the ref. He turned to the Ice Cats' left wing and ordered him to the penalty box.

Kyle was brushing the ice off his jersey.

"He hooked me first!" said the wing, pointing at Kyle.

"Go to the box, Anderson," yelled the Ice Cats' coach.

"I'm going," said the Ice Cats' wing. As he skated away, he gave Kyle a dirty look.

It's your own fault, thought Kyle.

The ref looked at Kyle.

"You get a penalty shot, Parker," he said.

Yes! thought Kyle.

Kyle skated over to the center circle where the ref had placed the puck.

Now's my chance, Kyle thought. *No one else is on the ice during a penalty shot. It's just the goalie and me!*

Kyle pushed off, and skated toward the goal. He crossed the blue line.

Back and forth, Kyle pushed the puck across the ice.

The Ice Cats' goalie stood near the edge of the crease.

Kyle faked to the right, and the goalie moved his body to the right too. *Gotcha!* Kyle hit the puck left.

Goal!

Sean skated over to Kyle. "Sweet goal!" he said.

"I'll bet Caleb liked that," said Kyle.

"He left," said Sean. "I saw him walking out right after you got tripped. He was on crutches."

CHAPTER 4

BAD NEWS, GOOD ADVICE

That night, when Kyle got home, he ran to his brother's bedroom. Caleb's door was closed. It always was. Kyle could hear loud music playing on the other side.

Kyle knocked.

"The door's closed," came Caleb's voice. "That means no visitors!"

"It's me," yelled Kyle.

"No visitors means no visitors," Caleb yelled back.

Whatever, thought Kyle. He turned the doorknob and stepped inside.

"Hey!" said Caleb. "I thought I told you to stay out!"

"What happened?" asked Kyle. He was looking at his brother. Caleb was sitting up on his bed, watching TV. His right ankle was propped up on a pillow. There was a thick bandage wrapped around it.

"You broke your ankle!" said Kyle.

"I told you not to come in," said Caleb.

"How bad is it?" asked Kyle. "When can you get back on the ice?"

Caleb's eyes were angry. "Please, Kyle. I said get out! Now!"

Kyle backed out of his brother's room. He closed the door just as Caleb threw a pillow at it from the other side.

In his own bedroom, Kyle lay down on the bed and stared at the ceiling.

What is Caleb going to do now? he wondered. The varsity team was important to him. He was the team's top scorer.

Kyle was about to turn off his bedside light when he heard a funny sound in the hall.

Stomp. Stomp.

Caleb appeared in the doorway. He had a crutch under his right arm.

"You got practice tomorrow?" asked
his older brother.

"Yeah," said Kyle.

Caleb frowned. "Lower your shot."

"What?" Kyle asked.

"When you take your shot," said
Caleb, "don't give the puck so much air."

"Cool," said Kyle.

Caleb turned and limped back to
his bedroom.

Kyle turned off his light. He kept staring at the ceiling. He replayed the night's game in his head, over and over.

"Hit it lower," he told himself.

CHAPTER 5

EAGLES VS. COUGARS

The next week, the Eagles played at home against the Cougars.

"Eric, Dave, and Kyle, I want you out on the ice," said Coach Williams. "The game is about to start."

Wow! thought Kyle. *I'm playing on the first line!*

"But, Coach," said Connor, "that's my line."

"I'm going to mix it up this time," said Coach Williams.

Connor turned and glared at Kyle.

I scored two goals in the last game, thought Kyle as he skated out onto the ice. *Connor didn't even have an assist.*

"Hey, it's nice to have a Parker on the first line," said Eric as he skated to the center face-off circle.

"Uh, thanks," said Kyle.

"Get ready to pass," said Dave, the right wing.

"You got it," said Kyle. He skated into position. It was time for the face-off.

The Cougars' center skated into the face-off circle. The ref looked at the clock. Then he nodded his head at the timekeeper.

"It's time, boys," the ref said. Then he dropped the puck.

Eric won the draw. *Bam!* The puck flew right. Dave received it right on the tape of his stick. The game was on!

Dave passed the puck back to Eric. Kyle, Dave, and Eric rushed over the blue line into the offensive zone.

Eric passed the puck to Kyle.

Oh yeah! thought Kyle. He moved closer to the goal. The Cougars' goalie backed into the crease. Kyle deked left and then passed the puck right to Eric. Eric blasted the puck into the net!

Goal!

The game just started, and I already have my first assist! thought Kyle.

He looked over at the bench.

Connor scowled at him. *What? I'm supposed to play badly so you can get back on the ice?* thought Kyle. *No way!*

"That was great," said Eric. "Let's do it again."

"Cool," said Kyle.

"Passing is how this line scores," said Dave.

On their next shift, Eric grabbed the puck on the face-off and passed it to Kyle.

Here we go, thought Kyle.

The Eagles' first line passed the puck back and forth several times as they moved into the offensive zone. Finally, Kyle caught the pass from Eric.

This is my chance, thought Kyle.

He snapped his wrist. The puck flew toward the net.

The goalie threw his body onto the ice and blocked the puck

Man! I almost had it! thought Kyle. *Maybe I should hit it lower next time, like Caleb said.*

He turned back toward the bench. Connor was smiling. Kyle couldn't understand why. *He's happy because I was blocked?* wondered Kyle.

Coach Williams called for a line change.

"You think you're cool, don't you?" said Connor as he came out onto the ice. "Just because you're a Parker. But you're big brother isn't so hot anymore with a broken ankle, is he?"

CHAPTER 6

PULL OUT

Kyle was angry. He had wanted to punch Connor, but he controlled himself. Getting into a fight wouldn't help him or the team. It wouldn't help his brother, either.

After a few more shifts, the coach called out the first line again.

Kyle looked up at the clock. The third period was almost over!

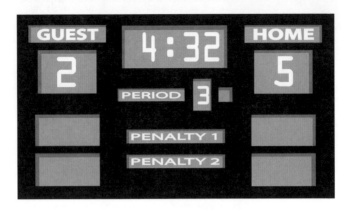

We're ahead five to two, he thought.

Eric won the face-off. Then Dave skated over and got the puck.

As long as Kyle was playing, he could forget about being angry at Connor.

The first line rushed into the Cougars' zone. Eric passed the puck to Kyle.

Yes! I see a hole! thought Kyle.

Kyle fired the puck toward the net. The goalie reached out his stick, and the puck bounced back out. Eric came in for the rebound. He slid the puck past the goalie. Goal!

The score was six to two. The Eagles were ahead.

At the next face-off, Eric was overpowered by the Cougars' center. The center caught the puck and rushed toward the Eagles' net.

Kyle raced to catch up with him.

Smoothly, the Cougars' line moved the puck back and forth between them.

We must be getting tired, thought Kyle, *or the Cougars are getting stronger.*

Dave tried to steal the puck, but the Cougars' wing kept it under control.

Closer and closer the Cougars skated toward the net. The Eagles' two defensemen moved in front of the goal.

A Cougar pulled his stick back. Slap shot! He scored.

BZZZ!

The buzzer sounded. The game was over with a score of six to three. The Cougars had made another goal, but the Eagles still won.

Eric skated around the ice with his stick in the air. Kyle skated over to give him a high five. *Whap!* Their gloves slapped in the air.

"I want Coach to make you part of our line," said Eric.

"We never scored this many points with Connor," said Dave.

"I heard that," said Connor. Kyle turned around. "You can't replace me," said Connor. "I'm not going to sit on the bench anymore!"

CHAPTER 7

SEAN'S PROBLEM

A week later, the Eagles were hosting the Archers. As the Eagles sat on the bench, Coach Williams looked up from his clipboard. "First line," he said.

Eric, Kyle, and Dave stood up and climbed over the boards.

"But Coach," said Connor.

"You played with Sean and Chris all week during practice," said Coach, "and it worked out just fine."

"He hogs the puck the whole time," muttered Sean.

"Then don't pass it to him," Dave whispered back to him.

"Yeah, right," said Sean.

As he skated toward the face-off circle, Eric said to Kyle, "Now our line is solid."

"It was six to three last week," said Dave. "Let's see if we can top that."

"No problem," said Kyle.

The Archers' first line was waiting for them at center ice. When the ref dropped the puck, the Archers' center pulled it back for his defenseman. Then the Archers' line skated toward the Eagles' zone.

"Where's the defense?" yelled Eric.

An Archers' wing rocketed over to the Eagles' net. The center set him up for a nice slap shot! Goal!

"Come on, men!" said Eric as he glided past Kyle. "Let's get it together."

The Archers won the next face-off too. This time, Dave spun around and stole the puck.

"Kyle!" he shouted.

Dave slipped the puck sideways to Kyle. Kyle caught it right on the tape.

Let's do this, he told himself.

Kyle skated toward the goal with Dave and Eric at his side.

Kyle saw a gap on the right side of the net. He passed the puck to Dave.

The goalie shifted his position, and then Dave slipped the puck back to Kyle.

Hit it hard and low! thought Kyle. He snapped his wrist.

Bam!

The puck slammed the back of the net.

Cool! A goal for me and an assist for Dave, thought Kyle. *Maybe I will catch up with Caleb!*

Coach Williams waved them in.

Kyle skated toward the bench. "Hey," said Kyle as Sean skated past, but Sean didn't even look at him.

What's his problem? Kyle turned around and watched as Sean skated over to the face-off circle.

Then Chris skated past Kyle without saying a word.

Connor shoved his face up to Kyle's.

"You can't take my place," said Connor. "I'm a better player than you are." Then he skated off.

Kyle skated back to the bench.

I'm helping the team win, he thought. *Why is everyone mad at me?*

CHAPTER 8

UPSET

The second period was about to start. Kyle skated onto the ice as the first line took their positions.

"It's so cool we're not playing with Connor anymore," said Eric.

"He hogs the puck the whole time anyway," said Dave.

"Sean's upset about it," said Kyle.

"Better him than me," said Dave.

Wham! Eric hit the puck out to Kyle.

Wow, Eric is really good, thought Kyle. *He's a better stickhandler than Chris ever was.*

Kyle caught the puck from Eric's shot and skated toward the goal.

Bam! An Archers' player slid up next to him and stole his puck.

I didn't even see that guy, thought Kyle. He glanced over at the coach, who was signaling him to keep his eyes open. Just behind the coach was Sean. Sean wasn't even watching the game.

It's not my fault I'm on the first line and Sean isn't, thought Kyle.

Kyle stopped thinking about Connor, Sean, and Chris. He put his mind completely on the game.

Swoosh! Dave flew in and stole the puck from the Archers' wing. He passed the puck to Eric. Eric slid it over to Kyle.

Kyle knew Eric was closer to the goal, so Kyle passed the puck back to Eric.

One of the Archers' defensemen swept his stick at the puck as Eric skated by.

The puck skidded across the ice.

Kyle skated after it and the Archers' players surrounded him.

"Get out of there, Kyle!"

Who shouted that? thought Kyle. It wasn't Sean or Coach Williams.

The Archers' center now had the puck. Kyle poke-checked the puck free. Dave picked up the puck and passed it back to Kyle.

Kyle spun around and sprinted toward the goal. He was on a breakaway!

All of the Archers' forwards skated after him. Kyle could hear their blades scraping the ice behind him, getting closer and closer.

Suddenly Kyle's foot got stuck. He fell forward onto the ice. "Tripping!" called the ref.

"I didn't trip him," said the Archers' center.

"Your stick is under his body," said the ref as Kyle picked himself up. "And he was in front of you. That makes it tripping."

"I don't believe this!" said the Archers' center.

"You want more time in the box?" asked the ref.

"Watch yourself next time," the center muttered to Kyle as he glided off.

The ref turned to Kyle and said, "You get a penalty shot."

Kyle nodded. He skated over to the center of the ice.

The ref set the puck. Kyle tapped it with his stick and began moving toward the goal.

This was how I made it to first string, thought Kyle. *It was that breakaway that showed Coach I was good enough.*

"Do it, Kyle!"

That voice again. Kyle looked over at the stands. It was Caleb, with a few of his buddies.

Caleb was standing up, holding on to his crutch, and waving his hand.

This time he's not leaving the game, thought Kyle.

The Archer's goalie backed into the crease as Kyle glided closer and closer.

The goalie's eyes moved back and forth, watching the puck.

Kyle searched for an opening. A small gap opened between the goalie's left skate and the net.

That was all Kyle needed.

Kyle took a deep breath. *Hit it low,* he told himself, remembering what his brother had said.

Whap!

Kyle hit the puck as hard as he could.

Nice and low.

The puck blasted past the goalie's skates and right into the back of the net.

Goal!

Caleb was holding his crutch over his head, waving it back and forth.

CHAPTER 9

BLOOD ON THE ICE

Kyle skated into position near the face-off circle. The game was almost over.

Eric and Dave coasted into place.

Kyle looked up at the scoreboard. Eagles 7, Archers 6. He had scored two of those goals himself. He also had three assists. One more goal and he would catch up with Caleb's totals for the season.

The Eagles won the next face-off.

Dave caught the puck and started skating toward the goal. Kyle and Eric followed. So did all of the Archers' forwards.

Kyle skated over to Dave's left. But before Dave could pass the puck, Kyle saw the Archers' center reach his stick out.

"Dave!" yelled Kyle. Too late. Dave tripped over the center's stick and tumbled face down onto the ice.

Kyle skated over and touched Dave's arm. Then he saw Dave's forehead.

"He's bleeding!" said Kyle.

Connor was mad. He came charging onto the ice, ready to start a fight.

Both benches emptied as players came out onto the ice. Sean grabbed Connor's arm. "Stop it, man!"

"You're not helping!" said Eric as he grabbed Connor's other arm.

Coach Williams and the Archers' coach ran over. "Back to the bench, Connor!" said Coach Williams.

"But—" said Connor.

"Make that the locker room," said the ref. "You're out of the game."

Connor stormed off the ice.

The ref turned to look at the Archers' center. "You're out too."

The Archers' center looked over at the bench. His coach pointed to the locker room.

Kyle moved aside so Coach Williams could look at Dave.

"Can you hear me, Dave?" asked Coach Williams.

Finally, Dave opened his eyes.

"Don't get up yet, son," said Coach Williams. He held up two fingers. "How many fingers do you see?"

"Uh, three," said Dave. "No, four."

"I think he has a concussion," said Coach Williams. "Help me carry him off the ice. His mom will need to take him to the doctor."

"Let me help," said the Archers' coach. The two coaches lifted Dave up slowly. They held on to the boy as he tried to stand up.

"Lean on me," said Coach Williams. The two coaches helped Dave off the ice. Dave's mom was waiting there.

Coach Williams spoke with Dave's mom.

Caleb and his buddies had come down from the stands and were standing close by the Eagles' bench.

"We can help, Coach!" said Caleb's friend Andy. Andy and his buddy helped Dave walk out of the arena. Dave's mom walked by their side.

Kyle wondered what would happen next.

CHAPTER 10

LAST PLAY

Ten minutes passed, and the Eagles' players were still waiting for the game to start again. Caleb turned to his brother. "Dave will be fine," he said. "It's time to get your head back in the game."

"This stinks," said Kyle. "Dave gets hurt, and Connor and Sean are mad at me because I'm on the first line."

"That's their problem," said Caleb. "Just ignore it. You got there because you're good."

"Yeah," said Kyle. "Thanks."

The players turned around as the two coaches and Caleb's buddies came back inside the arena.

"Will Dave be all right?" asked Kyle.

"He was talking in the car," said Coach Williams, "so he'll be fine. He just needs to be checked out by a doctor."

"We can go and see him tomorrow," said Sean.

Kyle turned around and looked at Sean. "We can both go tomorrow."

"But first we have to finish this game," said Coach Williams.

"Sean plays right wing," he said. "Okay, boys. Let's finish what we started."

Sean looked at Kyle and smiled.

The new first line skated out onto the ice. Eric skated into the face-off circle. Kyle and Sean took their places.

"We both got our wish, huh?" said Kyle.

"Yup, first line," said Sean.

The ref skated out with the puck and dropped it. Eric hit it out and Sean caught it.

Sean skated toward the goal and passed the puck to Eric. Eric skated into the offensive zone and passed the puck to Kyle.

Kyle hit the puck as hard as he could!

The puck sailed right between the goalie's legs.

BZZZ!

The game was over.

"Hat trick!" yelled Sean. "You got a hat trick!"

Eric skated over and gave Kyle a high five. "Three goals in one game!" Hats came flying onto the ice.

Sean slapped Kyle a high five too.

Kyle skated near the bench where Caleb was watching the game.

"You know how to play a good game, little brother," said Caleb.

"I have to," replied Kyle. "I'm a Parker boy, right?"

BLUE LINE BREAKAWAY

BLUE LINE BREAKAWAY

CHAPTER 1

IN THE DEFENSIVE ZONE

Jack Wickman stepped onto the ice and pushed away from the boards. His mouthguard dangled from the corner of his lips. Jack took a few strides toward the bench.

Coach Vorwald stood with his hands on his hips behind the glass. Jack couldn't quite look him in the eye.

"You're late, Wickman," Coach Vorwald said.

Jack nodded. "My sister had a game up north," he said. Jack knew saying that would get him off the hook. Everyone admired his sister.

"Right, big game coming up," Coach Vorwald said, nodding. "Warm up."

Jack scooped one of the pucks off the ice and practiced stickhandling. As he moved the puck toward the blue line, he thought of Becca. Even though his sister was five years older than him, Jack couldn't help feeling jealous.

Becca's skills were so impressive that coaches had moved her to the boys' team. *Yes*, Jack often said, *Becca's my sister. Yes, she plays hockey on the boys' team.*

For some reason, Jack usually had to give the info twice. *Yes, she's my sister. Yes, she plays for the boys' team.*

Ever since he could see over the boards, Jack had watched Becca in goal. Even then, he realized how good she was in front of the net. She could stop anything.

Now, Becca was a sixteen-year-old girl on the boys high school team, and Jack was getting tired of answering questions about her.

He wanted to watch from the ice, not from the boards. He wanted to stand out on his own. Jack was confident this year would be different. His sister was a goalie. He was a center. They both could be great players in their own way, and he intended to prove it.

Tryouts for the AAA Peewee team were about two months away. Jack hoped if he worked hard enough, he could make the team as a sixth grader.

WHEEE! WHEEE!

Coach Vorwald's whistle refocused Jack's attention. The coach tossed red jerseys to a handful of players, including Jack.

"Scrimmage time," said Coach Vorwald. "Red versus green. We're going to practice some dump and chase. Centers, Jack and Mason, I'll dump to the corner. Players, take your places."

Coach Vorwald dropped the puck, but there was no face-off in this drill. The puck landed with a thwack on the ice. Coach Vorwald turned and dumped it into the red team's offensive end. Jack and Mason raced to reach it first.

Mason used to be one of Jack's best friends. He was a good center but an even better winger.

The boys started out in Mites together and had been on teams together ever since. Mason had Jack beat on speed, but he couldn't match Jack's stickhandling.

Lately, Mason and Jack hadn't been seeing eye-to-eye when it came to hockey. Mason had talent but had started to get lazy and take shortcuts. He'd sometimes hang back and hope to get a loose puck instead of jumping into the play. He would try a slap shot from the corner instead of passing.

Jack was bothered by Mason's new style of play. Mason was cherry-picking.

Speed was speed, though, and Mason got to the puck that Coach Vorwald had dumped a second before Jack did. Jack caught up and was able to knock it away and get control.

He shot the puck out to one of the red team's defensemen and raced to the crease. The defenseman tapped it back. Jack deked Mason and tapped the puck through the goalie's five-hole for a sweet goal.

I'm Jack Wickman, thought Jack. *Not Becca Wickman's little brother.*

CHAPTER 2

REALITY CHECK

The next day, Jack walked to school.
In the lobby, a wall was painted to read
Home of the Warriors. Someone had hung a
life-sized poster of his sister. It read: *OUR #1
WARRIOR*. The poster put Jack in the dumps.

Megan and Brooke, hockey players from
the girls' Bantam team and friends of Jack,
walked up. They stood next to Jack. The
three of them gazed up at the poster.

"Pretty cool, huh?" said Brooke.

"Uh, I don't know," said Jack. "It might be too . . . big."

"I saw your sister's game," Megan said.

"Dude, she's awesome," added Brooke. "I bet she goes pro."

"Maybe," said Jack. He shoved his hands in his hoodie pockets.

"Dude, what's it feel like to live with a superstar?" Brooke asked.

"Super-duper," Jack replied.

Megan and Brooke laughed, not picking up on Jack's mood.

"Do you think she'll start on Friday?" Megan asked.

Jack shrugged. "We don't really have much time to talk during the season." he said. "Our game schedules and practice times are really busy. I have a game tomorrow, so I'm trying to concentrate on that."

Megan and Brooke stared at Jack.

"How can you not talk about hockey when you have a star in your house?" Megan asked. Her mouth remained open in disbelief.

"Dude," Brooke whispered. She placed her finger under Megan's chin and slowly closed Megan's mouth for her.

Before Jack had a chance to respond, Brooke chimed in, asking, "Will your sister be at your game? Do you think that I can talk to her about hockey?"

The bell rang, saving Jack from having to answer. He grabbed his backpack and headed toward class.

"Hey!" Megan called. "Want to practice some shots after school? Your mom's place?"

Jack turned, gave a thumbs-up, and then continued on toward class. He heard hurried footsteps behind him.

"Hey," Mason said. "Fifty-seven days."

"Yeah?" Jack said. He was confused.

"Until tryouts?" Mason said. "Man, Wickman. Get your head in the game."

Jack knew there'd be competition for the AAA Peewee spot, but he hadn't guessed Mason would try out. Mason's natural ability gave him a good chance to make it. But his recent bad habits . . .

The boys entered a classroom and sat.

Mason dropped his backpack on the desk behind Jack.

"Nice poster of your sister, by the way," Mason said. "I bet it feels familiar."

"What do you mean?" Jack asked.

Mason laughed. "Your sister being number one. You being number two."

Jack shook his head. It was a dumb comment. He pretended it didn't bother him.

CHAPTER 3

DRY LAND

Jack's mom lived in an apartment. In the parking lot, the landlord, Mr. Bakker, let the kids put a net up against the storage shed. Surrounding the net, black streaks and dents from poorly aimed pucks marked the side of the shed. Mr. Bakker likely knew he would have even more damage if he didn't have an area for the kids to practice.

With Mason competing for the AAA spot, Jack needed every spare moment he had to work on his skills. He planned on putting a few more dents in Mr. Bakker's shed.

Wearing full goalie gear except for the skates, Megan leaned against the lumber in the net. She lowered her facemask and then shuffled back and forth.

Jack carried a five-gallon pail of pucks. He dumped them on the ground in front of the net. That's where Megan was dropping to her knees to stop pretend pucks from getting into the goal. Jack picked up his stick and tapped a puck back and forth, moving it in front of Megan.

"So what's up?" Megan asked.

"What do you mean?" Jack replied.

"You're off your game," she said. "What's going on?"

Jack shot the puck in front of him toward the net. Megan stopped it with her blocker pad. She did a victory fist pump.

Jack spun his stick and slid another puck in front of him. This time he tapped the puck to his right and used a backhand to shoot toward the upper corner of the net.

Megan easily gloved the puck and then tossed it back to Jack. She did a second fist pump. This time she combined it with a dance move.

"Stop," Jack said. He tried not to smile.

Grabbing a different puck, Jack stepped away from the net. Megan had never shut him out on dry land practices.

Jack tapped his stick on the side of the puck, moving the puck to his left. He tapped on the opposite side of the puck and moved it to his right. Megan shuffled in the net, mirroring each move Jack made.

Jack slid the puck closer to the net. He lifted a quick wrist shot to the lower corner. Megan dropped to her knees and wedged her foot against the post. The puck bounced off her leg pad and rolled back toward Jack.

"Yooooooo-hooooo!" Megan sang as she dropped her stick and did a full victory dance.

Jack couldn't help but laugh. "Okay," he said. "I give up."

Megan smiled. "Now, what was going on with you today?"

Jack stared at the ground and moved a puck with the toe of his shoe. "Sometimes I get tired of people asking about Becca," Jack said. "I mean, I'm proud of her, but I skate too."

Megan picked at the tape on her stick and said, "Oh *noooooo*. The green-eyed monster."

"What?" Jack asked.

"It's my mom's saying for when someone is jealous," Megan said.

"Why?" Jack asked.

"No idea," said Megan. She shrugged. "But are you jealous?"

"Maybe," said Jack.

Megan took off her glove and wiped the sweat off her hand. She said, "You should have her back."

Megan's comment surprised Jack. Did people think he didn't have his sister's back? *Did* he have her back?

Jack slid a puck from the pile.

Megan put on her glove, squared to the puck, and relaxed her shoulders. "Just sayin', you know," she said.

Jack pulled back his stick and aimed high. When the puck zipped past Megan and pinged off the post and bounced in, Jack whooped. Then he dropped his stick and pumped his fist as Megan began to laugh.

CHAPTER 4

GAME DAY

Jack was happy to be back on the ice. Not only that, but two of the coaches from the AAA Peewee team were in the stands. The extra practice with Megan was paying off, and Jack was ready to show off his skill.

The buzzer sounded to end warm-ups. The pucks were cleared from the ice. All players except the starting lines skated to the bench.

Jack skated to center ice. The green and gold of his Warriors jersey stood out against the bright white of the rink.

The opposing center wore sport goggles and a red and black Jaguars jersey. He smiled at Jack and said, "Good luck."

Jack didn't know if he meant it or not.

A referee stood at center ice with a puck behind his back. The other players got into position. The ref signaled for Jack and the goggled center to prepare for the face-off. Jack leaned forward and lowered the blade of his stick onto the ice.

The whistle blew, and Jack fought for the puck. He won the face-off and knocked it into the defensive end to gain control. Jack skated toward the net as the two Warriors defensemen passed it back and forth along the blue line.

One of the players dumped the puck around the boards. Jack raced ahead of the opposing center and got to the puck first. Behind the net, Jack lost control when the Jaguars center reached him and blocked the puck between his skates.

Jack pushed himself between the center and the boards. The Jaguars center jabbed at the puck with his stick. Knocking the puck free, Jack was able to pass it to a Warrior waiting near the crease.

The winger backhanded the puck toward the goal's lower right corner, but the goalie gloved the puck. The referee blew the whistle, stopping play.

Jack readied for the next face-off. The referee waited for the players to line up. The goggled center moved forward over the hash marks.

"Square up," the ref said.

The Jaguars center backed up. The ref dropped the puck. Jack lost this time, and a Jaguars defenseman shot the puck into the neutral zone. A Jaguars winger batted the puck into the Warriors defensive end.

It was a two-on-one race to the goal. Elijah, the Warriors goalie, skated out to cut off the angle.

The Jaguars center shot the puck. The puck hit Elijah's leg pad and slid just out of the goal crease. Jack chased the play. He saw a Warriors defenseman out of position and raced to help Elijah.

The Jaguars center got his stick on the puck and shot before Elijah had a chance to recover. The puck went into the back of the net for a goal.

The Jaguars took the lead, 1–0.

The number one lit up in red under the GUEST side of the scoreboard. Jack looked up in the stands and saw his mom, dad, and sister watching the scoreboard. The two AAA coaches watched Jack for his reaction.

Jack whacked his stick against his shin pad. He skated to center ice and leaned forward with his stick across his knees. After the face-off, which he won, Jack hurried off ice for a shift change. He plopped down onto the bench.

Twice Jack watched as Mason had a chance to pass for a goal but took a shot instead. A third time, Mason waited at the blue line rather than going after the puck.

Mason wasn't the Warriors' only problem. As Jack watched, he saw skaters not covering on defense and wingers not helping out in the corners. Jack knew the Warriors had a tough climb ahead if they hoped to beat the Jaguars.

Coach Vorwald noticed the problems too. He signaled the players to huddle up between the second and third period.

"What's going on, guys?" Coach Vorwald yelled. "It's like you've never played together before. You're not covering the points. You're not hustling. Get it together!"

Some of the guys dropped their heads.

Coach Vorwald wasn't finished. "Mason," he said, "stop hanging back. The only good thing that happens at the blue line is a breakaway."

Coach continued, "Move your legs. Jack, shake off the goal. How about we see a little of your sister's toughness out there?"

Jack slouched lower on the bench.

"Hands in," Coach Vorwald said.

Coach Vorwald threw his hand out. Each player reached into the circle with a gloved hand.

"Team on three," Coach Vorwald said. "One, two . . . "

The Warriors shouted, "Team!"

Near the end of the third period, the scolding didn't matter. Both Jack and Coach Vorwald had been proven right. The game was still 1–0. Time was running out.

Play was stopped with one minute remaining on the clock.

As Mason skated to the bench, Jack called to him. "Mason, you have to pass sometimes," said Jack. "Don't be such a puck hog."

"You're not my coach," Mason said. The face-off was in the offensive end, and it was Jack's shift. His last chance.

Jack knew that the Jaguars goalie was a leftie. If Jack could get the puck out to the opposite side of the net, a winger might have a chance to tip it in.

The referee dropped the puck. Jack fought for it and got his stick on it. He tapped it to a Warriors winger.

The goal was open on the right side, and the winger took a shot. The goalie read the play, dropped to butterfly position, and blocked the attempt. A Jaguars defenseman scooped the puck and iced it to the opposite end of the rink.

Jack skated for the puck, but the buzzer sounded. The noise ended the game and ended Jack's hope for a big win. Jack looked up in the stands. The AAA coaches had already left the rink.

As Jack stepped off the ice, Becca was at the rink door. Jack shook his head when he saw her and walked in the opposite direction toward the locker room door.

CHAPTER 5

PIZZA AND SKEE-BALL

After the Warriors' loss, Jack shoved his gear in his hockey bag and headed off to find his dad, who stood waiting in the hallway. Mason waited next to Jack's dad. Seeing Mason stopped Jack in his tracks.

Jack thought about Mason's play on the ice. Jack realized he was still angry at Mason. Mason's scowl said he wasn't happy to see Jack, either.

"What's up?" Jack asked.

"Mason needs a ride home," said Jack's dad.

Jack slung his bag over his shoulder. He looked directly at the floor as he walked past his teammate.

"You guys hungry?" Jack's dad asked.

It was still early for a Saturday, and Jack was starving. But he shook his head. Jack didn't care to spend time with Mason.

"Starving," Mason replied.

"Luigi's?" Jack's dad suggested, ignoring Jack. Luigi's was the local pizza place. It was also Jack's favorite restaurant, mostly because of the awesome arcade.

"Sweet!" Mason said.

"I guess," Jack replied.

They rode to Luigi's in awkward silence.

When they arrived, Jack's dad said, "Pizza, then Skee-Ball." He dug quarters out of the cup holder in his car and gave the boys a handful of change.

Jack and Mason hurried inside.

As they sat together eating, Jack stuffed himself with pizza and mostly avoided talking. Afterward, they lined up quarters on the Skee-Ball machine.

"Highest score gets to pick dessert," said Jack's dad, dropping a quarter into the game. Nine balls rolled down the narrow wooden ramp. He rolled his first ball into the 100-point hole. After nine throws, he had scored 270 points.

Jack threw next. His first throw made the 50-point ring. After that, though, he seemed doomed to hit only the 10-point ring. Jack's final score was a low 130 points.

Mason threw last. His first three throws ended up in the 10-point rings.

"Playing it safe, Mason?" Jack's dad joked.

Mason laughed.

"Just like hockey," Jack said. "Mason finds the easiest way to score."

Mason pretended to laugh again, but Jack's dad stared at Jack. His dad was a relaxed guy, but he didn't put up with rudeness.

"Really hate to break it to you, pal," Jack's dad said, "but you weren't that hot on the ice today, either."

Jack's face went red.

"I think you owe Mason an apology," Jack's dad added.

Jack swallowed and coughed. "Sorry, Mason," he managed to mumble.

"I don't think I'm up for dessert," Jack's Dad said. "Becca's game starts soon anyway."

Mason stared at Jack. He put down the Skee-Ball, not finishing his turn.

CHAPTER 6

SHOOTING STAR

Jack sat alone at the rink. He watched from the stands as Becca worked the ice in front of the net. Over his shoulder, Jack saw Mason joke with a few Warriors teammates. Jack's dad stood at the top of the bleachers by himself, watching Becca.

Jack focused back on Becca. He watched as she blocked warm-up shots taken by her Warriors teammates. Once, a long-haired defenseman hit a slap shot at the same time as another Warriors skater. The puck came in high and bounced off Becca's helmet.

Becca dropped her stick and skated toward the long-haired kid. Jack could tell that she was angry.

Jack couldn't hear what was said, but he knew that it was heated. The long-haired kid had taken a cheap shot for some reason. *Maybe*, Jack thought, *just because she was a girl*. It made Jack angry.

Several of Becca's teammates joined her. One got between the long-haired kid and Becca. She glared at the kid as she picked up her stick and returned to the net.

Jack thought about how most of Becca's team seemed to have her back. *Teamwork*, Jack thought, *just add it to the list of things Becca does better than me*.

Back in the net, Becca squared up. The pucks came toward her again. She stopped nearly all of them. Clearly, Becca had a gift.

After a while, Megan and Brooke joined Jack in the stands.

"Hey, how'd the game go?" Brooke asked.

Jack shrugged.

"I heard Elijah had 27 saves. Dude, that's awesome," Brooke said. "What was the final?"

"We lost, one to nothing," Jack said.

"Bummer," Megan said. "So why aren't you hanging out with the team?"

Jack's shoulders slumped. He was too embarrassed to tell Megan the truth. His face turned red. "I don't know," Jack said.

Megan looked at Brooke. Brooke looked back at Megan. They both looked at Jack. The game soon began.

Midway through the first period, the game was scoreless. The Warriors' opponent, the Panthers, had been coming at Becca hard, and now a Panthers winger took another shot on goal.

Becca blocked it, and it deflected away.

Another Panthers skater swung at the puck.

Becca blocked this shot too and tried to cover the puck, but just then, the long-haired Warriors player slid into the crease. Clumsily, he knocked the puck loose in front of the net. The Panthers center quickly tapped it past Becca, who looked behind her for the puck.

Too late. Goal.

Jack's eyes widened. It should have been an easy save. Megan and Brooke hung their heads. Becca looked at the ceiling in disbelief.

As the game continued, the aggressive play was nonstop. The Panthers took shot after shot, and Becca stopped them all. All but one. By the end of the game, shots on goal were 37 to 21. Like Jack's Warriors, Becca's Warriors lost, 1–0.

Becca skated to center ice to congratulate the opposing goalie. Then she skated back to the net. She seemed calm until she smacked her stick against the post. Jack wasn't the only one who didn't like to lose. He hurried down the metal stands to meet his sister. Megan and Brooke followed.

Mason brushed by Jack. "Guess the Wickman family is zero for two," said Mason.

"What's your problem, Mason?" Jack said.

Mason glanced at Becca, who was watching the boys from behind the glass.

"Never mind," Mason said. "It looks like big sister is coming to the rescue."

Jack stepped forward and clenched his fists. He was ready to go at Mason.

Megan hopped between the two boys. "Dudes!" she said. "Don't."

CHAPTER 7

TEAMWORK?

"Something going on with your team?" Becca asked on the ride home with their dad.

"What? No," Jack lied.

Jack's dad threw a sideways glance at him.

"Is Mason bothering you?" Becca asked.

"No," Jack said.

"It's a really important year for me," Becca said. "I can't worry about you all the time."

For the third time that day, Jack felt angry. "It's a big year for me too," Jack said. "Maybe you should spend less time worrying about me and more time trying not to lose."

"That's enough," Jack's dad said. "Talk to each other when you can be respectful."

They rode the rest of the way home in silence. They ate dinner in silence. They went to bed in silence. Jack fell asleep that night without saying another word to his sister.

The next morning, both the anger and the loss hung over Jack's head. He wondered if he'd ruined his chances of making the AAA Peewee team. He wondered when his sister would talk to him. He wondered what would happen when he saw Mason.

Jack now knew that he needed to work on more than his hockey. He just wasn't sure how to fix the issues he was having with his friends. So he dove into the game. The AAA tryouts were in just a few weeks, so Jack practiced nightly. When he couldn't be on the ice, he practiced dry-land shots and worked out. To help his son build up leg muscle, Jack's dad had built a homemade slide board.

The board was a long and smooth ramp with deep edges. Jack would put on fuzzy socks and push himself side to side on the ramp. The slide board let him "skate" at home for more practice. The extra workouts helped. Jack felt himself beginning to catch up with Mason's speed.

One practice, while doing one of Coach Vorwald's speed drills, Jack beat Mason for the very first time. It was the first time Mason's talent wasn't enough.

Near the end of that same practice, Coach Vorwald called for a quick scrimmage. Ice time for the varsity team started next, so a few of the older boys were watching through the glass. Becca stood next to her teammates.

"Becca!" Coach Vorwald yelled. "Cover the other end."

Becca put on her helmet, stepped on the ice, and skated to the open net. Coach Vorwald threw red or green mesh jerseys to every other player. Mason was red. Jack was green.

"Becca's on the red team," Coach said.

Becca tightened her chinstrap. When she nodded, Coach Vorwald skated to center ice.

Mason and Jack faced one another and readied. Coach Vorwald dropped the puck.

The scrimmage was chippy from the start. Jack and Mason shoved each other out of the face-off. When Mason passed the puck to a defenseman, Jack checked him from behind, nearly knocking him off his feet. Mason's team regained control and passed to center ice. Jack blocked the pass. He stalled in the neutral zone to avoid an offsides call.

"Looking weak, Wickman," Mason said. He hip-checked Jack into the boards.

"Need another speed drill?" Jack replied.

Jack managed to slap the puck into the offensive zone. Mason took control. Jack chased Mason into the corner.

Becca hugged the post, watching them battle.

Fighting for the puck, Mason and Jack jostled for position. Jack knocked the puck free from the corner and tapped it to the crease.

Becca dropped to cover the puck. As she did, Mason ran into Jack from behind. Jack shoved Mason and accidentally elbowed Becca.

Becca fell backward onto the ice. Regaining her feet, she spit out her mouthguard. "You guys having fun?" she said. "'Cause I'm not!"

Coach Vorwald blew the whistle. "Jack, Mason, locker room," he said. "You're done for the day."

CHAPTER 8

BREAKING AWAY

It was the last game before tryouts, and Jack was running out of friends. Mason wasn't speaking to him. Becca was still mad. Megan and Brooke were being cold since he and Mason had nearly fought at the rink. It was a mess.

Jack had never played better or felt worse. Before the game, Jack and Mason sat across from each other in the locker room. Their teammates laughed and chatted. Mason laced up his skates. Jack taped his stick.

When it was time to warm up, the team filed out of the locker room and into the rink. Becca, Megan, Brooke, and Jack's dad watched from the stands. Jack knew he would need to try hard to focus on the game.

For the past week, Coach Vorwald had made both Jack and Mason skate laps every day after practice for the elbow to Becca. Coach probably hoped the two would work it out. They hadn't.

The opposing team, the Rebels, wore purple and white. After warm-ups, the bench players hopped the boards to take a seat while the starting lines huddled one last time.

The Warriors starters skated to center ice. Jack cleared his head. He took his spot in the face-off circle. The Rebels starting center, a guy with braces but no mouthguard, faced off against Jack.

The Rebels center won the face-off and was able to dump the puck. Jack back-checked hard and hustled toward the play. The braces kid and a Warriors grinder fought for the puck in the corner.

A Warriors defenseman dumped the puck into the neutral zone. Jack chased the puck for a blue line breakaway.

He would have a one-on-one showdown with the goalie if he hustled. The braces skater tried to catch up.

Jack dangled the puck and waited for his chance. When the goalie opened his legs, Jack flicked the puck with a light touch. The puck shot through the goalie's legs for a five-hole score.

GOAL!

Jack high-fived a Warriors defenseman.

From the cheering crowd, Becca and Jack's dad gave Jack a thumbs-up. Except for Mason, all the Warriors, including Coach Vorwald, were pumped up.

Jack won the next face-off again and dumped the puck down ice. He hurried to the bench for a shift change. Mason hopped the boards to the ice. The puck whizzed past Mason. A Rebels winger and Mason got tangled up. Mason went head over skates.

Mason's gloves, stick, and mouthguard scattered across the ice. It looked like a yard sale.

The referee blew the whistle, stopping the play. Mason gathered up his things and skated to the bench.

The third-line center hustled onto the ice for Mason, and Mason sat next to Jack on the bench.

"You okay?" Jack asked.

"That," Mason said, "was embarrassing."
He slid down the bench away from Jack.

The Rebels and Warriors were evenly
matched. After two periods, the Warriors still
held a 1–0 lead. During a third period break
on the bench, Jack realized that he wasn't the
only one who had improved. His teammates
were all getting better.

That included Mason, who was digging
in the corners and actually hustling. The
Warriors got their second goal of the game
thanks to Mason. He faked a shot and froze
the goalie before passing it to a teammate,
who scored.

The game ended with a hard-fought 2–0
Warriors win. Jack knew he was ready for
Peewee tryouts. But he still felt like something
was off.

CHAPTER 9

IN THE ZONE

After the game, some of the players went to Luigi's to celebrate. Jack wanted to go home.

Their dad drove Jack and Becca as the two sat next to one another in silence.

"Remember when I said I can't worry about you this year?" Becca asked.

"Yeah," Jack said.

"I'm worried," Becca said.

"Yeah," Jack replied and dropped his shoulders. "I've been a jerk. I'm sorry, Becca. Are we good now?" he asked.

"We're good," Becca said.

Becca smiled. Jack knew he was forgiven.

"Any idea how I make it right with my friends?" Jack asked.

Becca thought for a moment. "I think I might," Becca answered.

* * *

The next day after school, Jack felt more nervous about seeing his friends than he had been for the game. He and Becca had come up with a plan. Jack asked Becca to invite Megan, Brooke, and Mason over to the apartment. Jack knew they would have a hard time saying no to his sister.

Megan, Brooke, and Mason met Jack out by Mr. Bakker's practice shed. When they arrived, Becca awaited them in full goalie gear, in the net.

Becca looked at the group and asked, "May I practice with you?"

Megan, Brooke, and Mason stared at Jack wide-eyed.

"I've been a jerk," Jack said.

"Totally," Megan said.

"A major jerk," Brooke said.

Mason looked at the ground. "I may have been part of the problem," he said.

"*May* have?" Megan asked.

"Dude," Brooke said to Mason.

"Okay. I am part of the problem," Mason said. "Sorry, Jack."

"Me too," Jack said.

"Ugh, are we done apologizing?" Becca asked. "Are we going to practice or what?"

Megan, Brooke, and Mason whooped and hollered. Becca invited Megan into the net to give her some pointers.

Mason, Brooke, and Jack passed back and forth. After Megan was warmed up, the others took shots.

"Move forward to cut off the angle," Becca said to Megan. "It makes it harder to score."

Megan took a step into the crease and caught the next shot in her glove.

"Nice," Becca said.

Mason and Jack practiced passing back and forth. Brooke kept firing shots at Megan.

Becca stepped into the net.

"Your turn, Jack-O'-Lantern," Becca said.

"What?" Megan asked.

"Did?" Brooke asked.

"She?" Mason asked.

"Yes," Jack said, laughing. "She called me Jack-O'-Lantern."

"*Awwwww*," the group said all at once.

"Yeah, yeah," Jack said. He scooped a pile of pucks toward him and prepared to shoot.

"Line up your shot, Superstar. Or do you prefer Hot Shot?" Becca asked.

Oh, it was on. Jack lined up the puck as if he was ready to shoot.

Becca got into position. "Where would you shoot?" she asked.

"Top corner," Jack said.

"Now, get down on the ground and look at the net from the puck," Becca said.

Megan, Mason, Brooke, and Jack took turns getting down to look up from the puck.

"Now where would you shoot?" Becca asked.

"Probably between your blocker and leg," Jack said. The others nodded in agreement.

"Where do you look?" Megan asked Becca.

Becca said, "Always at the puck, but sometimes at the ice in front of the stick. Almost never at the player."

Megan nodded.

Each player took turns shooting on Becca, but none even got close to the net. They practiced for more than an hour. They were having so much fun, no one noticed the time. Jack's mom approached the group and said it was time to call it a night.

"Two more minutes?" Becca asked.

Jack's mom zipped her coat and watched them continue to shoot.

Jack lined up his final shot for the night and tried to imagine what the shot looked like from the ground. Jack pulled back his stick and lowered his grip.

He brought down his stick with all of his power. The flat of his blade connected with the puck. It was the fastest slap shot he'd ever hit.

His mouth dropped open when he realized the puck made it into the net. Becca threw up her arms in celebration, and the entire group cheered. Mason punched

Jack's shoulder, and Brooke patted his back. Megan tossed her gloves into the air.

"That's what I'm talking about!" Becca said.

"Thanks, Chew-Becca," Jack said.

"Did?" Megan asked.

"He?" Brooke asked.

"Say?" Mason asked.

"Yes," Becca said.

"*Awwwwww,*" the group said all together.

CHAPTER 10

AAA DAY

Tryouts. Just two spots open on the AAA team. More than fifty kids took the ice with several adults watching them play.

The skaters were divided into groups of ten and started with skating drills. After the drills, the coaches added pucks to judge the players' stickhandling skills. Jack handled the drills with ease. Mason occasionally let a puck get away from him but always seemed to recover.

Finally, the coaches set up four-on-four plays. Again, Jack and Mason were paired up. Jack was happy they had a chance to work together on the ice. During the scrimmage, Jack played as center and Mason played as winger. The two passed easily back and forth.

Not once did Mason slow at the blue line. Instead Mason pushed past a defenseman and shot the puck around the boards.

The other winger player was able to pick up the puck and send it into the slot where Jack was waiting. Jack looked for an opening and shot toward the five-hole. The goalie dropped into butterfly position, but it was too late. The puck was in the net!

Mason patted Jack's helmet. "Good job," Mason said. He smiled.

"Thanks," Jack said. He felt relieved and happy. "Nice pass."

The coaches took the puck back to center ice and whistled to start play again. Tryouts lasted about an hour. Jack left the ice tired. He'd done his best.

* * *

A few days later, Jack made his way to the rink after school let out. The list for the AAA team would be taped next to the door at the rink. Becca's game was about to start, and he wanted to see the results before the game.

Jack walked into the lobby. The entryway was mostly empty, except for Becca. She stood in her game gear next to the tryout list.

She smiled and pointed to Mason's name on the AAA team. Then she beamed as she moved her finger up the list to Jack's name.

"You know, I didn't make the AAA team until the seventh grade," Becca said.

Jack's eyes widened. "No way," he said.

"Nice job, Wickman," Becca said, checking Jack with her shoulder.

"Thanks, Becca," Jack said, following his sister into the rink.